DANCE ALL NIGHT

Praise for Alexis Daria

Praise for *Dance All Night: A Dance Off Holiday Novella*:

"*Dance All Night* is the perfect little gift from Santa you didn't know to ask for."
    —LaQuette, author of the Queens of Kings series

"A holiday romance that will dance straight to your heart, overflowing with romantic feels, ultra-sexiness, and a hero you'll wish you could take home with you."
    —Robin Lovett, author of the Planet of Desire series

"*Dance All Night* had me from the first Lindy Hop."
    —C.L. Polk, author of *Witchmark*

Praise for *Take the Lead: A Dance Off Novel* (#1):

2018 RITA® Award Winner for Best First Book
    Named one of the Best Romance Novels of 2017 by *The Washington Post* and *Entertainment Weekly*

"A sparkling debut." —*Entertainment Weekly*

"Vibrantly written." —*The Washington Post*

Praise for *Dance with Me: A Dance Off Novel* (#2):

"The passion Daria has for this world is palpable in every word...and one hopes she has many more love stories to tell within it."
—BookPage

Praise for Alexis Daria:

"An author who clearly adores the world she's developed—and the characters she's matched."
—Sarah MacLean, *New York Times* bestselling author of *Wicked and the Wallflower*

"A charming and authentic voice."
—Sonali Dev, award-winning author of *A Distant Heart*

DANCE ALL NIGHT

A DANCE OFF HOLIDAY NOVELLA

ALEXIS DARIA

Dance All Night: A Dance Off Holiday Novella

Copyright © 2018 by Alexis Daria

Print KDP ISBN: 9781731283405

Print BN IS ISBN: 9781641970716

NYLA Publishing

121 West 27th St., Suite 1201, New York, NY 10001

http://www.nyliterary.com

Dedication

For Howard and Claudia. I can't thank you enough.

About this Book

This holiday novella is set in the world of *The Dance Off*, a TV dance competition that pairs celebrities with professional dancers. Aside from the first chapter, *Dance All Night* takes place after the events of the first two books, *Take the Lead* and *Dance with Me*. While the characters from the previous books show up briefly, this story is written as a standalone and can be enjoyed even if you have not read the others in the series.

Chapter One

New Year's Eve, last year

Hangovers and early flights didn't mix well for Nikolai Kovalenko. And since he was getting on a plane first thing the next morning, he'd been sucking down seltzer with lime all night. As a result, the poolside bar at his brother Dimitri's annual New Year's Eve bash was completely out of the stuff, and the mini water bottles were gone, too. The bartender offered him tonic, but Nik turned him down. He could just go inside for a glass of water.

The party was at Dimitri's house, and Nik knew his way to the kitchen well. After all, he lived here, too, though not for much longer. But Mitya—as Nik had called Dimitri for as long as he could remember—didn't know that yet, and Nik wasn't sure when to break the news. Dimitri would never admit it, but Nik knew his brother liked having him around, even though Nik was often away on touring productions of Broadway shows for long stretches of time.

In the kitchen, Nik spotted one of Mitya's coworkers from *The Dance Off*—Jess Davenport, a professional ballroom dancer —and gave her a nod in greeting. He didn't know her well, but they'd met a few times before. She had dark eyes that sparked with humor, smooth brown skin, and a nimbus of black curls. She was petite, probably one of the shortest female dancers on the show, but with a strong, athletic build—currently showcased to perfection in a strapless silver cocktail dress.

Her ass was planted on the breakfast counter, and she was eating potato chips right out of the bag. He raised an eyebrow at the chips—there were servers circulating outside, offering food catered by Dimitri's restaurant.

"I wanted something salty," she said with a shrug.

Nik took a glass down from the cabinet and filled it from the filter spout by the sink. "I wanted some water."

From outside, raised voices began counting down from thirty. Nik shot a glance at the microwave clock. 11:59.

Jess picked up the open bottle of champagne next to her on the counter, probably left over from pouring the toast—the toast they were missing. Lifting it to her lips, she said, "Well, cheers, I guess." And took a swig.

Twenty-five, twenty-four...

Almost midnight. Another year gone. Nik would be twenty-seven next year.

Outside, people laughed and cheered drunkenly as they counted down together. If he ran, he could join them.

But...why? Most of them were his brother's friends and colleagues anyway. Some of them would be pairing off to garner a kiss at midnight, adhering to the superstition that *not* kissing someone meant you'd be lonely for the rest of the year.

Well, Nik was leaving the next day to rehearse his role as a dancer in the national tour of *Seize the Night*, a musical about rival vigilante gangs. And with the whirlwind that was life on the road, he didn't have time to be lonely.

Then again...why tempt fate?

Nik set down his water and sent Jess a shrewd look. "Hey. You single?"

Jess lowered the champagne bottle and scrunched up her brow. "Yeah. Why?"

He jerked his head to the side, indicating the revelers counting down to midnight. "Wanna kiss?"

Her lips pressed together like she was holding back a smile. Narrowing her eyes, she swept him with an appraising once-over.

Seventeen, sixteen…

Whatever she saw in him passed muster. She crooked her finger, beckoning him over, but didn't hop down from the counter.

The saucy look in her dark eyes and the sexy little finger taunt had his pulse speeding up. What had started as a friendly, almost bored suggestion, built in anticipation as Nik crossed the kitchen to her and stepped into the space between her parted knees.

"I was just eating potato chips," she reminded him, licking her fingertips. The innocent move sent a curl of arousal through him.

"I don't care." He took the champagne bottle and gulped some down. The bubbles raced across his tongue, invigorating and tart. A little wouldn't hurt. And anyway, he had the feeling it would be worth it.

Eight, seven…

"Sour cream and onion," she said, reclaiming the bottle for another sip before setting it aside.

"Still don't care." Nik stepped in closer and slipped his arm around her waist.

He met her gaze, waiting for midnight. Hers held amusement, and her lush lips curved just a little as she draped her arms over his shoulders. She smelled like cherries.

Three, two…

One!

He kissed her.

Happy new year!

The cherry scent was from her flavored lip balm. He caught the barest taste of it, the sweetness combining with lingering salt from the chips. Then her mouth tilted, her lips parted beneath his, and he took her up on the invitation to go deeper, to slide his tongue against hers. She tasted like champagne, or maybe that was him. And like champagne, she went right to his head. He wanted to lick her up, down, and all over. But all he'd asked for was a kiss.

His other hand, which had been gripping the edge of the counter tight, came up of its own volition and cupped the back of her neck. His fingers massaged her there. She was so smooth, so warm. Her arms tightened around him and her back arched, pressing her hot little body into his.

Just a kiss, he reminded himself, but then she nipped at his bottom lip with her teeth and sucked on it.

Groaning, he fisted his hand in the back of her dress, but he couldn't pull her any closer than she already was.

A sound in the doorway made them both look up, and half a second later Dimitri burst in.

"Whoa, sorry." Mitya threw up his hands, then pointed at the fridge. "I just—ah…" He opened it, grabbed a jar of olives, and hurried out.

Nik turned back to Jess. His pulse pounded and his lungs heaved like he'd been running. "Thanks," he said.

Stupid. He could've kicked himself. What the hell kind of thing was that to say to a woman after she'd just kissed the hell out of you and made your knees go weak?

Jess just smirked, the corner of those delectable lips pinching together and revealing the barest dimple in her cheek. "My pleasure."

Keeping her eyes on his, she unwound her arms from his neck and traced her hands down over his shoulders and chest in slow, lingering touches. The smoldering heat in her eyes made his muscles tighten. Then she hopped down from the counter, but since he hadn't moved back yet, the front of her body slid straight down his. Shit, she could probably feel that he was getting hard. He stepped away to give her space. She sent him a sultry look, then picked up the champagne and chips and gestured to the doorway with them. "Ready to go back to the party?"

He licked his lips, tasting cherries, salt, and her. He was ready for something, but it wasn't the party. Her kiss had rocked his world, but this was already more than he'd bargained for. He liked his life as it was, and he wasn't looking to have it shaken up right now. "I'm, uh…I actually have to finish packing."

It sounded like an excuse, and maybe it kind of was, but he really did have to pack.

Her brow furrowed, and the last vestiges of fire left her eyes. "Packing? Where're you going?"

"Leaving tomorrow to start a national tour," he said. "First stop is Chicago for rehearsals."

She blinked. "Oh. That's where I'm from."

He raised his eyebrows. As much as he wasn't looking to go further, he did want to know more about her. "Yeah?"

She rolled her eyes. "I couldn't wait to get away. Came to LA the first chance I got."

"I get it." He stuck his hands in his jeans pockets, since he didn't know what to do with them. Or, rather, to stop himself from doing what he wanted to do—to hold her and kiss her again, then see where it went. But the vibe had slipped into easy, friendly banter, and he didn't want to ruin it. "All I want to do is travel."

"Nah, dude. I didn't say that. I did more than my fair share of traveling while in the competitive ballroom circuit. I just wanted to get the hell out of Chicago and settle somewhere else."

Settle. What a strange concept. For him, New York City was home. While he hadn't been born there, it was where he'd grown up, where his parents still lived, and it would therefore always be home to him. Los Angeles was another home base, because Dimitri lived here. Beyond that? Settling was the last thing he wanted to do. "Why?"

Her eyes shuttered and her shoulders slumped just a fraction. "Too cold," she said, her tone deceptively breezy, and he knew it wasn't the whole truth.

He wanted to ask more, but he was leaving in the morning, and he hadn't lied when he said he loved traveling. For as long as he could remember, he'd wanted to get out into the world and experience everything it had to offer. He'd been born in Ukraine, but had spent all of his youth in Brooklyn. Lots of people couldn't understand why he wanted to leave New York, but for him, the city was all he'd ever known. So, he booked dancer roles with touring productions that let him get away, all in the pursuit of adventure.

"Well, you picked a nice city to settle in," he said. "Can't beat Los Angeles weather." It had been a warm winter so far. And he couldn't believe he was talking about the *weather*.

Jess squinted at him. "Why did you say 'settle' like it's a dirty word?"

He was caught off-guard as his mind supplied other dirty words. "Huh?"

"You said 'settle' like it was something gross you'd scraped off your shoe," she said, nudging him with the champagne bottle. "What's up with that?"

Since she was poking him with it, and since her observation was a little too on the nose, Nik took the bottle and drank. "The idea of settling down somewhere doesn't appeal to me," he finally replied. Something about her words gave him a hot, uncomfortable feeling, like his skin was too tight. "I want to see the world, go on adventures. I don't want to get stuck in one place and become complacent, you know?"

"Ah. You have wanderlust." There was a decisive tone to her voice, like she was delivering a diagnosis. She grabbed the bottle from him. "Well, thanks for the kiss. Good luck with your *adventures*." She said *adventures* like it was a curse. And then she sailed out of the kitchen, leaving him with half a hard-on and her salty-sweet taste on his lips, questioning his own convictions.

Chapter Two

_____

11 1/2 months later…
December 16th

"We should go to the party."
Jess looked up from the fundraiser plans spread out on the desk before her. Naomi Simpson, her bestie and one of the counselors at Starlight House, a group home for at-risk adolescent girls, bustled into the little office. Her smile was wide, and her usually cool-toned brown skin was flushed.

"What party?"

"The one your friend Rhianne is throwing tonight." Naomi perched on the edge of the desk, her butt wrinkling some of the papers.

Jess couldn't say anything, since technically it was Naomi's desk and Naomi's office, and Jess was just a volunteer here. The room was small, but it had a window and a shelf overflowing with plants. Jess preferred working in here to the plain, boring conference room, but even that would have been preferable to what Naomi proposed.

"Oh. That party." Rhianne Davis was another pro on *The Dance*

Off and one of Jess's closest friends from the reality dance competition show. "It's a sexy ugly sweater party, and you know how I feel about gimmicky holiday shit. Besides, I'm not going out tonight. I have a date."

Naomi huffed. "Jess, you can't date a cable box, and even your DVR deserves a night off."

"Dating is overrated." Especially in Los Angeles.

"You're too young to be so jaded." At thirty, Naomi was like Jess's California big sister. Except she was closer to the older woman than she was to her own real sister, Jaina, who was the same age as Naomi but lived in Texas.

"You need to play a little more," Naomi went on. "Have some fun. Go out. Whenever *The Dance Off*'s season ends, it's like you shut down."

"That makes me sound like a robot," Jess grumbled.

"If the cyborg shoe fits…" Naomi shrugged. "All work and no play makes Jess Davenport a big ol' curmudgeon."

Jess slapped a hand on the papers. "Are you calling me a Scrooge?"

"Maybe."

Jess couldn't argue. Maybe she did become a homebody during the off-season. Aside from leading fundraising efforts and dance classes for Starlight House—and catching up on her DVR—there was no hustling, no partying, and definitely no dating in her schedule. Trying to find a boyfriend in Los Angeles was a hot mess of games and ghosting, and she was fucking tired of it.

As a counselor, it was possible Naomi had picked up on Jess's mood. If Jess were being honest, she had been feeling a little stuck lately. Work was the only thing in her life going right, but she had no idea what her next steps were. Or should be. Or even what she wanted them to be. Aside from working on *The Dance Off* and volunteering at Starlight, she just wanted to chill. And that did not include ugly sweaters, sexy or otherwise.

But Naomi wanted to go to the party, and since Rhianne was Jess's friend and coworker, that meant Jess had to take her.

"Fine," she said with a sigh, shuffling her papers into a folder. "We'll go."

Naomi cheered and pumped her fist. "Lucky for you, I have a plethora of Christmas junk we can wear."

Jess hid her face behind the folder. "Oh, *joy*."

A few hours later, dressed in a green t-shirt with "Lit As a Christmas Tree" emblazoned across the chest, Jess showed up at Rhianne's craftsman-style house with Naomi at her side.

Naomi had not been kidding about her Christmas t-shirt collection. Jess had vetoed a red tee with "Ho³" on it, and another that showed a plate of cookies with the words, "I Put Out For Santa." You thought you knew a person, and then you found out they had *that* in their closet.

Naomi had opted for a red tee that said, "Naughty Girls Get More Presents," and added a Santa hat over her long box braids. Yeah, she looked cute, but Jess had drawn the line at the sparkly plush antlers Naomi tried to push on her.

Oh, lord. Speaking of antlers…

Rhianne rushed over to greet them, her dark auburn curls floating around her like a wispy cloud. "Jess! I'm so glad you could make it," she gushed, the words extra charming in her Australian accent. Her rosy skin glowed with excitement, alcohol, and a fair helping of glitter smeared on her cheekbones.

"Um…thanks…" *Look away look away look—*

It was no use. Jess stared openly at Rhianne's chest. Well, at one side of it, anyway. Luckily, Naomi picked up the thread of conversation and introduced herself. She seemed completely unbothered by Rhianne's appearance, as if it were the most normal thing in the world.

Rhianne wore a red tank top, but part of it was missing. One of her pale breasts was bared, and it was…decorated. Like Rudolph the Red-Nosed Freaking Reindeer.

A sparkly red pastie covered Rhianne's nipple, but attached to the tip was a round, glittering red "nose." Above it, two googly eyes had been stuck to Rhianne's bare skin, and above *those* were a pair of brown felt antlers.

"I need a drink," Jess muttered. It was the only way she'd survive this night.

"I'll show you where the bar is set up," Rhianne chirped, and herded them toward the dining room like a good reindeer hostess.

"I don't think I can do this," Jess whispered to Naomi, who had the nerve to laugh.

As they moved through the party, Jess scanned the crowd for familiar faces, waving to the people she knew as she followed her friends to the bar.

One face in particular caught her eye and she froze, breath seizing in her chest.

Unbidden, a hot flush of desire unfurled in her belly.

She grabbed Naomi and Rhianne to bring them to a halt and spoke from the corner of her mouth. "Remember that guy I kissed at New Year's Eve?"

Naomi frowned. "Yeah?"

"And remember how I said he's been leaving heart emojis on all my social media posts over the last few months?"

"So romantic," Rhianne said with a sigh.

Jess didn't say so, but she thought it was sweet, too. "Well, he's here."

Rhianne squealed. Like, straight-up squealed with delight. "Ooh, where is he? Do I know him?"

"Um, yeah." Jess squeezed her eyes shut. "He's Dimitri Kovalenko's younger brother."

"*Nik?*" Rhianne grabbed Jess's arm, bare left breast jiggling. It took all of Jess's power not to stare at her friend's Rudolph boob, despite the fact that *it* was staring at *her*. "Nik is the one who kissed you last year?"

"Yep." Or was it this year? Technically this year, since it had happened after the clock struck midnight.

"Where is he?" Naomi craned her neck, grilling everyone at the party with an eagle-eyed glare.

"Over there." Jess pointed surreptitiously across the room to where Nik chatted with his brother, Dimitri, one of the former judges on *The Dance Off*.

Rhianne leaned in close, and that damn Rudolph nose tapped Jess's elbow. She held back a flinch. She had no problem with boobs, but boobs dressed up with reindeer faces were creepy as fuck. "Are you going to kiss him again?"

Naomi leaned in on the other side. "You should totally kiss him again."

Jess scrunched up her shoulders and stepped away from both of them before Rudolph could bite her. "How the hell do I have devils on both shoulders? Isn't Christmas about angels or some shit?"

Rhianne scoffed. "No. Christmas is about parties and presents. Obviously." She gestured at the revelry around them.

Despite her defensiveness, Jess eyed Nik speculatively. No, she definitely wouldn't mind kissing him again. He wasn't very tall, maybe five-foot-ten, but she was so petite that super tall dudes made her look like a child when she stood next to them.

Nik was a nice, normal kind of tall, with a body that was anything but normal or nice. He had the kind of build that would make her grandma drool. Broad shoulders, lean muscles that were cut and sinewy, and a sense of boundless energy about him. The ballroom guys she'd grown up around were strong but slim, and the ones on *The Dance Off* tended to bulk up more for TV. Nik was a different sort of dancer, one used to leaping and bounding across the stage. He seemed to take on shows that required a ton of physicality and movement.

Okay, so she'd looked up his work history. And fine, yes, she had stalked his social media, too.

It wasn't just his body that appealed. He had a nice face, too. Amber brown eyes that could easily be described as "soulful," if one were the romantic sort, which she was *not*. Brown hair with a tendency to curl. An olive-toned complexion and an easy smile, bright against a few day's growth of dark facial hair. He kept it trimmed neat and short, but she'd seen from his pictures that he sometimes shaved it, depending on the role.

She knew the beard was soft, though. And his lips. Mmm, his lips. Those were soft, too.

Liquid heat rolled through her. Damn it. Yes, she *so* wanted to kiss him again. And maybe more.

Okay, jeez, who was she kidding? *Definitely* more.

"Looks like you're thinking about playing with his jingle bells," Naomi said suggestively.

"Don't be gross." Still, Jess grabbed a mint and her cherry lip balm from her purse. She wasn't going to seek Nik out, but if he found her, what would it hurt to be ready? Just in case.

———

NIK HAD ARRIVED at Rhianne's party with his brother and his brother's girlfriend Natasha, decked out in homemade ugly sweater chic.

Most of Nik's stuff was still in storage, so any weirdo Christmas attire he might have once owned was unavailable. He'd officially moved out of Dimitri's house over the summer, despite the fact that he was currently staying in his old room during this visit.

Dimitri and Natasha didn't own Christmas sweaters, either, so they'd all hit up the craft store that morning and spent the afternoon making their own outfits. Tash wore a green tank top with fake poinsettias and holly hot-glued to it. Mitya had rigged a battery pack to some colorful Christmas lights and wrapped them around his black velvet blazer. It was oddly fitting for a guy who always wanted to be center of attention.

Mitya and Tash had seemed to be having fun together while crafting, so Nik had just grabbed some accessories and left them to it. As a result, his costume was pretty simple.

"Don't hit on Rhianne," Dimitri warned Nik. "She's the hostess."

Nik called him a rude name in Russian. "I don't *hit on* women. I'm nice to them. It's different."

Anyway, Nik had no intention of hitting on Rhianne. His whole reason for being at this party was to hopefully see Jess again. He hadn't reached out to her over the summer, when he was last in LA, although he'd thought about it. But then again, a few months ago he'd been content to travel the world, indulging the wanderlust Jess had accused him of and giving no thought to settling down. He'd always felt like he was searching for something, and if he could just travel enough, meet enough people, have enough experiences, he'd find it. But now, the search just didn't interest him the same way it once had.

Dimitri rolled his eyes, but Natasha nodded.

"It's true," she said. "He just treats women like people. But he's so handsome, it seems like flirting."

"Spasibo, sestra," Nik said, making her smile. Tash had been studying Russian for a few months, so she understood simple phrases like "thanks, sis."

Nik suspected Dimitri was probably going to marry Natasha sooner rather than later. She and Dimitri had worked together on *The Dance Off* for years, dating on and off before Natasha finally moved in with him a few months ago. Since then, Dimitri had mellowed out, and it was nice to see him happier and not as brooding. It made Nik wonder if all that traveling, all that searching, was just keeping him stuck in "search" mode. If he was fixated on the search, he wasn't going to find whatever he was looking for. Maybe he had to settle first, so he'd be ready when it showed up for him.

It didn't help that when he thought of settling down, his brain automatically replayed the kiss he'd shared with Jess on New Year's, and the conversation after.

There was something there, something between them, and he didn't think it was one-sided. He hadn't imagined the way she'd responded to his kiss, and he was still kicking himself for turning down her invitation to go back to the party with her. They could have spent the rest of the night dancing, getting to know each other, maybe cuddling and kissing more.

He'd never know.

In the last few months, ever since Nik had found out that the *Seize the Night* national tour was ending in mid-December, he'd been trying to give Jess hints. He'd liked all her Instagram posts—mostly promo and behind the scenes shots from *The Dance Off*, along with dance classes she taught, yoga poses, and the group home where she volunteered—and left brief comments with lots of emojis, but she wasn't biting. He hadn't wanted to push it, since he'd been away and didn't want to come off like a creep. But now that he was back in LA, he wanted to see her in person, to find out if they really did have the spark he'd felt all those months ago. When Mitya had told him about this party, he'd figured there was a good chance Jess would be here, too.

Nik accepted a beer from Dimitri, raised the bottle to his lips, and then…there she was. Right there, standing at the other end of the house, chatting with two other women. A rush of emotion overwhelmed him, comprised of every good thing—joy and light and sparkles, and the sugary-sweet scent of cherries.

That kind of feeling didn't come along often. Hell, he'd been chasing it for years, to no avail. He needed to follow it. Because *this*, this feeling, was what he'd been searching for all along. His brother might tease him for being a romantic, but Mitya could probably confirm that this was how you felt when you saw someone and just *knew* you were meant for each other.

He shoved the beer back into his brother's hand.

Mitya glanced at him, startled. "What, you don't want it?"

Nik didn't answer. Instead, he launched himself through the crowd, dodging dancers and actors in all sorts of ridiculous getups, his eyes focused solely on Jess. The closer he got, the more his heart sang in his chest.

Yes. Yes. Her.

Yeah, he was a fucking romantic. Who cared? When it was right, it was right.

He stopped behind her, grinning like a fool. "Jess."

"Nik!" She turned, surprise and pleasure on her face, and gave him a small smile. "Hi."

God, she was pretty. The last time he'd seen her ran on a loop through his mind. He said the words he'd spoken to her then, with a slight variation, hoping she remembered.

"Hey. You still single? Wanna kiss?"

Her eyes widened, her nostrils flared, and both of her friends sucked in their breaths with loud, excited gasps. One of them was Rhianne, and…was that her tit? What the heck was—?

Jess rolled her eyes and grabbed his hand. "Come on, you. We've gotta talk." Then she dragged him away from her friends, who collapsed into giggles behind them.

Well, shit. So much for being charming.

———

HOLDING HIS HAND, Jess pulled Nik away before he could say some other foolish thing in front of Naomi and Rhianne. *Lord.* She was never going to hear the end of it from them now.

Nik's hand was big, his fingers strong but gentle as they gripped hers. How was it that she knew the shape of his mouth, but not his hand?

Jess had been to Rhianne's house plenty of times, so she knew the layout. She led Nik into the hall just outside Rhianne's office, but didn't go inside. Locking them in a room together would lead to kissing, and she wanted to talk to him first.

Once she was reasonably sure they were alone and not likely to be overheard, she crossed her arms and tilted her head at him, sending him an "explain yourself" glare.

He just grinned at her, a silly, sweet grin that made her feel warm all over. Damn, this man was just too attractive.

And…what was he wearing?

His white sleeveless tank showed off arm muscles made for licking, but he'd also hooked a couple small red Christmas tree baubles onto it. The dangling ornaments—positioned right over his nips—had tiny bells attached that jingled when he moved.

It was utterly ridiculous. But somehow completely sexy. And, thank goodness, there were no Rudolph faces in sight.

"Hi," he said.

"Hi yourself. What was that all about?" She jerked her head to the side, indicating what he'd just said in front of her friends.

"Ah, that." Cheeks red, he rubbed the back of his neck, making his bells tinkle. That adorable boy blush threatened to weaken her resolve.

"I saw you," he continued. "And then all I could think about was the *last* time I saw you and what I said then. Do you remember—"

"Yeah, I remember." How could she forget a kiss like that, and the moments leading up to it? She'd wanted to keep going, to rub herself all over him, but then he'd announced that he was leaving the next morning. The kiss had been fun, but that was all. No chance for anything more.

Just like all her other attempts at forming a meaningful romantic connection.

"So, that's it?" she said. "You wanna know if I'm still single and down for fucking around before you leave again tomorrow?"

He held up both hands and shook his head with a vigorous motion. "No. Not at all. I mean, I *do* want to know if you're single, but not for that reason. And I'm not leaving tomorrow."

Not tomorrow, but likely at some point. Since her arms were already crossed, she crossed them tighter. "What reason, then?"

Taking a deep breath, he spoke slowly, like he wasn't completely sure about what he was doing. "I...really liked kissing you. And talking to you."

She raised an eyebrow. His awkwardness was endearing as fuck, and it was hard to stay annoyed at him, but she needed to sort this out before it went any further.

Nik's shoulders hunched a bit, like he was embarrassed, and the rest of his words came out in an earnest rush. "I haven't been able to stop thinking about you, Jess. All year. I want to see if this thing that I feel... Well, I want to know if you feel it, too. And if so, then...let's give this a try."

He paused, waiting for her to speak, but his shy, stilted declaration of intent had stolen her breath and her voice.

This was, by far, the most romantic thing that had ever happened to her in all her twenty-three years. Who didn't like having a handsome, sexy man tell you he liked you? But it was also unexpected and, she could admit, more than a little overwhelming.

"What's 'this'?" she finally asked.

He waved a hand between them. "Us."

Us. As if they were already an *us*, a *them*, a unit. Nerves tangled with excitement inside her. But the nerves reminded her that this wasn't someone who'd stick around. Hell, he'd already taken off once before. After planting a panty-melting kiss on her, he'd basically said, "Sorry, gotta pack," and shipped off. And while she was down for another brief lip lock with him, she wasn't about to get emotionally invested.

In her experience, people their age—and all the guys she'd dated in the entertainment industry since moving to Los Angeles when she was twenty—just wanted to play games in between gigs. How many times had she heard it before, after her heart was already involved? *This is just for fun. You knew that, right?* And then they were gone—to the next show, the next performance, the next woman. She was a magnet for fuckboys.

And Nik was no different.

"What's with all the heart emojis?" she asked, changing the subject and trying to keep her tone stern so he wouldn't see how much he'd already affected her.

He cheeks turned red again. "I'm not allowed to like your pictures?"

She planted her hands on her hips. "Whatever you're up to, it's not happening. You wanna kiss again right now? Fine. You're a great kisser. But that's it. You shrugged me off last year, and I'm not about

17

that 'girl in every port' life, buddy. If you think I'm gonna sit around waiting for your ass to show up and then drop everything when you decide you wanna play, you've got another thing coming."

His gaze was intent, like he was really listening to her every word and considering what she said.

"I don't want that either," he said, and damn if his voice wasn't sincere. "You deserve better than that."

She raised an eyebrow, covering the rush of pleasure his words gave her with a sheen of always-reliable attitude. "So, what *do* you want?"

He spread his hands. "We're both off work for a little while. Let's make the most of it—spend time together, get to know each other better."

"To what end?"

The look he gave her was so intense, she almost swallowed her tongue. "As far as you're willing to go."

What was he saying? Would he stay in Los Angeles—for her? According to his social media posts, he'd been having a blast traveling the great wide world. She shook off the mushy feelings his words inspired. He talked a good game, but she wasn't about to make this mistake again.

"How do I know you're not going to run off again? Your wanderlust is alive and well, and people don't change overnight."

"You're right." He inclined his head to concede the point. "It hasn't been overnight. It's been over the last few months."

Since he'd started his campaign to court her on social media, she guessed. The sudden attention had both confused and charmed her. She hadn't known what to make of it, but she'd also looked forward to seeing his name pop up in her notifications.

Still, he'd been off on tour, so she'd simply clicked "like" on the comments and moved on.

Rather than tell him all that, she shook her head. "Listen. You're sweet, and you're cute as hell, but I don't believe you."

"What can I do to convince you I'm serious?"

She huffed out a laugh. "Dude, that would take a mother-fuckin' Christmas miracle."

Right before her eyes, his energy shifted and his whole body perked up. Damn, he must be amazing to watch on stage. He could so clearly convey emotion with his entire being.

"A Christmas miracle?" He said it like it was a real thing within his reach.

"Yeah. And I don't believe in those, either."

Now, his brow furrowed. "Why not?"

Jess rolled her eyes. "Are you telling me you do?"

He shrugged. "The holidays are a special time. Everyone tries just a little bit harder to be good, to be helpful, to be compassionate. Isn't that a miracle?"

Lord, spare her from idealists. But his optimism tugged at her, urging her to agree. She slammed a mental lid on the impulse and made her voice extra flippant.

"I don't know. I hate the holidays."

If she'd punched him in those rock-hard abs, he might have looked less surprised. "You what?"

She huffed. People always gave her nonsense about her stance on winter holidays. "Look, I've got nothing against Arbor Day. But Christmas? Not for me. I mean, I'll go to parties, like this one, because I like my friends. But I don't buy into the rest of it. It's just a marketing tactic so retailers can make their bottom line before the end of the fiscal year."

He raised a dark brow. "That's a very cynical view of the most magical time of year."

A smile tugged at her lips. "I can't help it if I lost my rose-colored glasses. Or green and red, as the case may be."

"Aha. So, you're a Scrooge."

"Why does everyone keep calling me that today?" She shuffled her feet against the hall carpet.

"All right, how about this?" Nik's voice took on a cajoling tone and he clasped his hands together in front of him.

She eyed him warily, sure she wasn't going to like whatever he said next. "How about what?"

"Since it'll take a Christmas miracle to get you to believe that I'm for real about exploring something serious with you—and you don't believe in Christmas miracles—if I can get you to believe in the magic of the holiday season, then, by extension, you will *also* believe that I'm not playing games with you."

She blinked at him a few times, charmed in spite of herself. But she was too contrary by nature to give in that easily. "That didn't make any freaking sense."

"Sure it did." He put out his hand to shake. "Just give me three dates—three *holiday-themed* dates—to change your mind. About me *and* Christmas."

Staring at his hand, Jess was filled with the urge to say yes. To believe him. Not about the Christmas stuff, but to believe that someone liked her as much as he claimed to. Liked her enough to go to all this trouble.

Liked her enough to stick around.

But she didn't. This would still be a game for him, an entertaining way to pass time over the holidays before his next adventure.

If it was a game, though...maybe she could have fun for a bit, too, like Naomi had been pushing her to do. Maybe it *was* time to play a little. Just for the last days of the year. And then he'd be off wherever his next gig took him, and she'd go back to her regular, boring life.

Alone.

She pushed the thought away.

"Fine," she said, clasping his hand. "Three dates."

His grin lit up his whole face, and she felt it inside her, too.

What the hell was she getting herself into?

Chapter Three

December 18th

For their first date, Nik asked Jess to meet him at the Americana at Brand, an outdoor mall in Glendale designed to look like someone's fantasy version of a European village. For some reason he couldn't understand, the mall also had apartments on the upper levels, and he had to pass through an open-air concierge area on his way in from the parking garage.

A trolley, festooned with wreaths, holly, and an enormous glittering red bow, wound its way around the track circling the "town square," where an enormously tall, conical Christmas tree drew the eye upward. Red and white lights hung in abundance from the boughs of the trees ringing the square and over the walkways. The air smelled like cinnamon, and tinkling, jazzy music scores from classic Christmas movies played unobtrusively in the background.

Having grown up in Brooklyn, Nik found the Americana both bizarre and quaint. He hoped Jess would feel the same. He couldn't imagine a more magical setting for a date. Even better, it was *warm*. Doing holiday stuff in New York City was fun, but made harder by actual winter weather. He wore a light jacket, because the temperature in LA dropped at night, but he didn't need a scarf, hat, or gloves.

Part of him missed the whole ritual of getting ready to go out in the cold. But only a very small part.

The sun was going down as he waited for Jess by one of the fountains, where a giant, nearly naked gold man froze mid-prance in the center, surrounded by cheerful jets of water colored by tiny lights in the fountain's base. Red and green, of course.

As the minutes ticked by, Nik worried that Jess wasn't going to show up. He'd arrived early, just in case he hit traffic, and because it would've been rude to be late. But what if she'd just been humoring him to get him to leave her alone? Maybe he'd read the whole situation all wrong.

Then he spotted her coming toward him, and his face broke into a grin. She wore a gray bomber jacket and jeans. A turquoise patterned headscarf pushed her curls into an updo. Nik waved, and she joined him by the fountain.

"Traffic on the 2." She rolled her eyes, but leaned in to give him a half hug.

He'd take it. She smelled like cherries, reminding him of their first kiss, and when he put his arm around her, her petite frame fit perfectly against him.

She peered around them, taking in all the over-the-top holiday décor, and pouted those pretty lips in a way that said, "I'm here, but I'm not happy about it." Nik couldn't help but laugh.

"Bah humbug?" he asked, and her mouth compressed to hold back a grin.

"You said it, not me." She moved closer and slipped her arm through his. The alternating colors of the fountain's lights reflected on her hair—green, then red, then green again. "So, what are we doing on this date?"

"Well, one of the main tenets of the holidays is giving gifts to loved ones."

She huffed out a laugh. "I know what Christmas *is*. I'm just not a fan of celebrating it."

Her words made him wonder why, but it was too soon to ask.

"Let's start with some shopping," he suggested, trying to keep things light.

"Who says I plan to shop for anyone?" She side-eyed the passing trolley and its waving conductor.

"Maybe this was all just a ruse to get you to help me buy gifts for Natasha and my cousin's wife."

That got a chuckle out of her and she elbowed his side. "Pretty elaborate ruse, my dude. But I should probably get a gift for my agent while I'm here. Let's start over there."

Jess directed them to a makeup store, and Nik followed her lead. As they browsed the spa and skincare aisles, he told her about his family—his mother and father back in Brooklyn, who'd moved their whole family from Ukraine to America in the 1990s; his brother, who was learning the meaning of the word "compromise" with Natasha; his cousin Alex and his wife, Marina, who were expecting a baby in the spring; and his cousin Fedya, Nik's partner in crime when they were little, who was now a father of three.

Nik was careful to open up first. He hadn't forgotten how, after their first kiss, she'd ducked his question about why she'd left Chicago. He seriously doubted "too cold" was the only reason. So as he spoke, he kept his comments thoughtful, leaving spaces and gaps for her to step in, if she wanted to. And he didn't ask her anything outright.

Eventually, she opened up just a little.

"My sister Jaina's an accountant in Texas," she said, testing a red lipstick on the back of her hand.

He waited to see if she'd supply more info. After turning her hand this way and that, as if checking how the lipstick looked in the light, she continued.

"She's a drama queen. Every time we talk, Jaina has some other shit going on with her job, her friends, or a man. I can't keep up."

"Is that for her?" he asked, pointing at the lipstick.

"Hell no. This is for me." She added two more stripes of red in different shades and compared them. "Which one do you think is better?"

Nik flagged down a salesperson to help Jess try on the color she liked best, and he smiled as she preened in the tiny mirror attached to the end of the aisle.

"I like it," he said. "Very Christmassy."

"Shut up. No, it's not." But she sent him a coy little smile that set him ablaze.

"What's the color called?" he asked, because he wanted to remember it.

She rolled her eyes to the ceiling and sighed. "Holly Jolly Berry."

Nik laughed, and as they wound their way toward the cashiers, Jess surprised him by returning to the topic of family. Her words came out in bursts, laced with unspoken—and perhaps unacknowledged—emotions.

"I mean, it's great and all that you have a good connection with your family," she said. "But not everyone has that. And the holidays force the issue, like there's something wrong with you if you're not in the spirit of celebrating and putting aside your differences to deal with your toxic or dysfunctional family members."

He couldn't argue with that. "So, how do you usually celebrate, if not with your family?"

"I stay home and catch up on TV, indulging in some good old R&R while everyone else is busy."

"Alone?" He tried to keep the surprise out of his voice, but probably failed.

"Yes, *alone*. I like my 'me time.'"

Nik wanted to ask more, to dig deeper into what she was saying, but she'd tell him when—and if—she was ready.

"Oh, Naomi would love this." Jess picked up a skin-care boxed set. "She has sensitive skin, so she's always on the lookout for all-natural products. I'm going to get this for her."

"Is she the one who was at Rhianne's party with you?" Her

energy changed when she talked about her friend, as opposed to her family. She lit up when she mentioned Naomi's name.

"Yeah, and now I'm never going to hear the end of it, thanks to you."

"The end of what?"

"She's one hundred percent in favor of us kissing again."

"Can't say I disagree." He smiled when her lips quirked. "What's your opinion on the matter?"

"I'm still deciding," she answered haughtily. She tossed the package into the basket he carried, and they moved on.

Outside, he begged her to pose for cheesy pictures with him in front of every Christmassy backdrop they passed, including the trolley.

"Where are you posting these?" she demanded.

"Nowhere. They're just for me."

"Oh." She was quiet a moment. "Well, text me the best ones."

He did it on the spot. Then, he directed her to one of the snack stands set up around the fountains. "No holiday outing is complete without hot chocolate."

She held up her hands and spread her fingers, as if to indicate the lack of gloves. "You drink hot chocolate when it's cold. It's not cold. It's sixty-two degrees."

He pretended to be affronted. "Miss Jessica Davenport, we are *adults* and we can drink hot chocolate anytime we damn well please."

His remark got her laughing, and she gave his gut a light whack…that ended in a furtive caress. Was she feeling him up? He didn't mind that at all.

As they waited in line, he peppered her with trivial questions.

"Marshmallows or whipped cream?"

"I can't have both?"

"Peppermint or caramel?"

"On what? Never mind. Caramel. Always caramel. Anything mint-flavored makes me think of toothpaste."

"Tea or coffee?"

"I am not a morning person, so give me *all* the coffee."

"Gingerbread or chocolate chip?"

"What kind of monster do you think I am? Chocolate chip."

He adored the way she never answered a question with a simple yes or no, A or B. Every time she opened her mouth, her personality spilled out along with her words. She might not know it, but she was sharing more of herself than she realized.

Once they had their drinks, they sat at a small café table and sipped.

"Good?" he asked.

"Mmm." She closed her eyes and savored. "So good."

She had a tiny bit of whipped cream on her lip. He ached to lick it off. Instead, he pointed, and her own tongue darted out to catch it.

Almost as good.

She drank more of her cocoa, watching the people around them as he watched her. Her prickliness guarded a heart that had been hurt. He didn't know how or when, but he'd have to work extra hard to change her mind and show her that he'd changed his.

He hated that their conversation eleven months ago had been about his refusal to be tied down, and now, that was all he wanted. Cheesy as it sounded, he wanted to tie them together with a big Christmas bow.

How could he make her believe that if she didn't want to?

The music filling the outdoor area changed from a slower Christmas ballad to a rollicking jazz-style carol. The beat zinged through Nik, demanding he get on his feet.

"Now what?" Jess asked, her tone suspicious. "Your whole body just lit up like…well, like a damn Christmas tree."

"Let's dance." He took her hand.

"What about our drinks?" She gestured at their mostly full cups. "They'll get cold."

"I'll buy you another one."

He handed their shopping bags and a twenty dollar bill to one of the concierge guys on the lawn—yes, this mall had those. "Hold these for me?" When the guy nodded, Nik took Jess's hand and drew her out onto the main road that wound around the center lawns.

"Nik!" She laughed out his name, but didn't look embarrassed or resistant. He'd never heard a better sound. "No one else is dancing."

"I know." He grinned and pulled her into a close hold, with his right hand resting on her left shoulder blade, and his left hand gently clasping the fingers of her right. "We're about to make a spectacle of ourselves."

———

"WHAT KIND OF SPECTACLE?" Jess couldn't have wiped the grin off her face if her life depended on it. His enthusiasm was infectious, like a disease borne on the smell of pine and Christmas cheer.

"You like Lindy hop, right?"

She loved it. "How'd you know?"

He gave her a patient smile. "Jeshka, I've seen every single one of your Instagram posts. I'm a fan."

"Oh." Her cheeks warmed at the thought of him following her photos all year, paying enough attention to note and remember something like this, instead of passively double-clicking to heart a picture and moving on. Then the way he'd said her name caught up to her. "Jeshka?"

"My people live for nicknames." He raised his eyebrows and looked over her shoulder. "I hope you're okay with going viral."

"What?" She peeked behind him. Sure enough, several shoppers already had their phones out and pointed at where she stood with Nik. This would probably end up all over social media, was likely being live-streamed this very moment, with their names tagged soon if not already. Speculation was bound to arise about whether or not they were dating.

Whatever. Let them watch. She had nothing to hide. Someone

might even think it was a publicity stunt, like a flash mob. It could only help both of their careers.

Not only that, Nik was an amazing dancer. Right now, she just wanted the experience of dancing with him.

What would Naomi say?

Go play.

"Let's do this," Jess said, and Nik took that as his cue, stepping them into the dance with his left foot.

The song was a modern big band hit, with jazzy vocals and a lively percussive beat punctuated by blaring trumpets. Nik deftly led her through the eight-count pattern of the Lindy swing out —*rock step, triple step, walk, walk, triple step*—matching the song's fast-paced rhythm with speed and control.

Dancing with Nik was like being caught in a bubble—just the two of them, with a perfect, almost telepathic connection between their bodies and the music. He communicated moves to her through the tension in his fingers holding hers, the touch of his hand on her upper back, and shifts in balance. Dance created a language only spoken between the partners, as intimate as it was invigorating.

Despite all her Scrooging, tonight was the most fun she'd had in a very long time. Giving herself over to the dance and the boppy beat, Jess sank low in her knees, twisting on the balls of her feet as she swiveled left and right. The road was so well paved, her flat tennis shoes slid easily on the surface. She even closed her eyes at one point, letting the music and the steps—and Nik—take over. The soft scent of his cologne plied her memory, bringing to mind the feel of his mouth on hers. Her body warmed, and it wasn't just from exertion.

The song's vocals dropped out, launching into an instrumental interlude, and Nik led her into a tuck turn for a Tandem Charleston. Facing out, with her back to his front, she noticed the crowd growing around them. The awareness of their audience, combined with the heat emanating from Nik's body and the connection she felt through their joined hands, sent a thrill racing through her.

As they kicked their way into a swing out, Jess couldn't hold back—she let out a huge laugh, and Nik's answering grin made her melt inside. The chorus returned and they sank down, preparing to lift with their knees. A second later, Jess was going up, both feet lifting off the ground in a perfectly controlled frog jump. Her spirit soared with the movement. She freaking *loved* this dance.

The crowd *oohed*, but she ignored them, the entirety of her attention fixed on Nik's wide smile.

And he, of course, was focused solely on her. As he had been all night.

No denying it. She hadn't had a date this good since—probably ever.

The problem was, Nik was going to leave again. Eventually, his wanderlust would return and off he'd go, just like all the other guys she'd dated in this industry. This dancing around, talking about their families and being sweet together…it was only getting her in deeper.

Deep wasn't fun. Deep would lead to heartbreak when he left. Because he *would* leave. They always did.

Except right now, she didn't care. If the spirit of the holidays was about believing in things you had no proof of, well…then that's what she'd try to do. Maybe Nik was right and there was something real between them. Or maybe he was just playing her. But dancing was about being in the moment, so she let everything else wash away on a tide of trombone moans and swivel steps.

They rocked and kicked and jumped and twirled their way through the rest of dance, a flurry of movement that felt like sheer perfection. When the song ended, people clapped. There were tons of phone cameras pointed their way. They bowed for the assembled crowd, then Nik drew her away and back toward the hot chocolate stand.

As they walked, Jess pressed her warm fingertips to the taut muscles of her cheeks. She was grinning like a damn fool and breathing hard, but so was Nik. He met her eyes, his chest heaving. A flippy sensation happened somewhere in her ribcage.

Oh.

Oh. No.

He'd done it. Just like that. He'd wormed his way in and won her over already. If she were being honest with herself, he'd been doing it since last New Year's Eve. The kiss, the heart emojis, the insistence on holiday cheer. Who could resist all that? Not her, that was for damn sure.

She had to try. She should try. Or…for now, she could just enjoy it. For a little while. She'd still be her snarky self on the outside, but inside…

She'd soak it all in, holding these warm, gushy feelings tight. So when he left, she'd remember, at least for a short while, how it had felt.

Nik collected their purchases from the concierge and bought new cups of hot cocoa, as promised. Then they sat at a different table to drink.

"You're good," she said, finally catching her breath after a sip of the rich, sweet cocoa.

He shrugged. "I do what I can. We can't all be swing dance champions, like you."

"What, did you Google me?"

"Of course I did. Didn't you Google me?"

She pressed her lips together, not wanting to answer, but his expectant eyebrow lift teased it out of her. "Yes, damn it. I did."

He threw his head back and laughed, eyes crinkling at the corners. It was a nice sound, light and masculine.

"You've done Broadway," she said, because it was something she'd read about him and wanted to know more about. Why did he join touring productions when he could be on the biggest stage of all?

"I have."

"So, why tour?"

He fiddled with the plastic lid of his drink. "You already know why."

"The travel and *adventures*?"

He hunched his shoulders, cringing as she reminded him of his own words from nearly a year ago. "It seemed important at the time."

"Is it because you're from New York?"

"Partly." He kicked out his legs and reclined as much as the flimsy chair would allow, folding his hands over his flat belly. "Don't get me wrong, it's still a relentless struggle to get those roles. You have to put in the time, the effort, and be one hundred percent dedicated. But when you can stay at your parents' house in Brooklyn for free and your brother is a movie star with a memorable—and by that, I mean *foreign*—last name, it's not quite as hard as it is for other people."

She gave him an exasperated look. "Are you saying you went on tour because getting roles on Broadway was too *easy* for you? Because if you are, I might have to throw this hot chocolate on you. And then you'll have to get me a *third* one."

He shifted in his chair like he wasn't comfortable with the topic. "It's not that it was easy, it was that I felt...I don't know, *stuck*. Like I hadn't progressed at all as a person. As a dancer, sure, I was constantly learning new things. But as a...god, this is going to sound cliché."

"Go on. I'm sorry, I won't make fun." Because now she was into it, imagining a younger version of Nik, living at home and wanting...more.

She understood that feeling. And she didn't know what to do about it, so if he had an answer, she wanted to hear it.

"As a man." He rubbed a hand over his face, and she caught the telltale red tinge on his cheeks. That sexy, sexy blush.

He dropped his hand and continued. "I'm a younger brother, by a lot of years. As long as I was at home, I was still the baby. Maybe you get it, because you have an older sister."

She nodded. "Oh yeah, I feel you on the awkward family

dynamics. Why do you think I moved out so early? I was twenty when I came to LA."

"And how long ago was that?" he asked with a grin.

"Three and a half years, and don't you dare make a joke about me being younger than you, because you are not *that* much older than I am, okay?"

He held up both hands, chuckling. "I won't, I promise. But you sure have done a lot in a short amount of time."

And because he was so easy to talk to, it all came spilling out. Her LA story. How she'd started dancing young, with tap and hip hop, before finding ballroom dance through an extracurricular program in middle school. How she'd racked up junior championships in ballroom and swing while living in Chicago, then decided moving to Los Angeles was the next step.

If only she could figure out what came next *now*.

"Why did you switch to ballroom?" he asked.

She closed her eyes, remembering. "I fell in love with the Viennese waltz the first time I saw it performed, thanks to a class trip. It was so smooth and romantic. From there, I became obsessed with old movies and big dance numbers. Those led me to swing. When I found out about the Lindy hop, I researched the history and learned that it started in Harlem. I was hooked."

She fell quiet, remembering. Ballroom had been so different from everything she'd ever known for those first thirteen years, when her whole life had been harsh angles and words. Ballroom dance was sweeping curves and intimate connection between the couple and the music. It was, at her core, all she ever wanted.

"I couldn't wait to get away," she went on. "Outside of the dance crowd, I didn't have too many friends. I traveled a lot for competitions, and none of my classmates understood what I was doing—or why. So I never really felt like I belonged there, you know?" She chuckled, but it was with a bittersweet pang. It had taken time, but she could look back with compassion at the lonely girl she'd once been. "I was probably the only teenager in Chicago with pictures of Billie

Holiday and Norma Miller, the 'queen of swing,' taped to my walls."

"Hey, look who you're talking to. We had framed photos of Baryshnikov and Nureyev in our living room, like they were part of the family."

"At least your family was all into it. Your mom was a dance teacher, right? My parents just thought I was nuts. They wanted me to be a nurse or something else with reliable job security."

They'd supported her desire to dance, footing the bill for ballroom lessons, costumes, and travel when she started competing and winning, but they hadn't understood it as a calling or a career until she'd appeared on TV. Now, they were her biggest fans, voting for her every week that she was in the competition, but the memory of those early years still carried a dull ache.

"So, how did you get on *The Dance Off?*" Nik asked. "It's a pretty sweet gig."

She waved a hand dismissively. "I auditioned for a backup dancer spot on a whim. I didn't think they'd hire me."

"Why not? You're an amazing dancer."

Jess tugged on the end of one of her curls and let it bounce back. "My hair. I stopped chemically straightening it after I quit competing, and you don't see a lot of natural hair in the ballroom dance world. But the producers liked my moves and the range of dances in my repertoire, plus they were willing to bring on a new stylist for me. I couldn't turn it down."

"I'm glad you didn't. Otherwise we might never have met." Nik's phone beeped, and he checked the screen. "Come on. It's almost time."

"Time for what?" But she let him take her hand and lead her along the trolley path. Other people were moving in the same direction, and when the clock hit seven, she understood why.

A noisy whirring filled the air, and as she looked up to find the source of the sound, wonder and surprise had her jaw falling open.

"Nik, is that…is that *snow?*"

He grinned down at her. "You didn't know they do this here?"

She shook her head, watching in amazement as clusters of tiny flakes flew off the roof and into the dark sky over the shoppers. Around them, children squealed, and even the adults made delighted murmurs. Snow in Los Angeles was impossible, yet here it was.

Nik would say it was the magic of Christmas. And even though she knew it was a marvel of technology, part of her thought he might be right.

She held out a hand to catch some of the flakes, inspecting them on her palm. "What's it made out of?"

"Snow."

She shot him an amused smirk. "No, really."

He heaved a sigh. "You want me to ruin the magic?"

"I just want to know."

"It's a foam. Like tiny bubbles, I guess."

The "snow" dissolved on her hand. "It's amazing. Floating in the air like this, it looks just like the real thing."

"It's weird, isn't it?"

"What is?"

"That it's not cold. If you're used to real winters, it's weird to see snow when it's not cold. At least, I think so."

"Yeah, I get what you mean." Just the sight of the snow made her want to cozy up to him for warmth...or for the pleasure of cuddling with that hot bod.

In total, the snowfall lasted all of five minutes. When it was over, Jess turned to Nik. The twinkling fairy lights reflected in his eyes. "Okay," she said in a soft voice. "I guess that was pretty magical."

The smile that eased over his features was pretty damn magical, too, and set her heart to thumping in her chest.

He stepped closer, and even though they were surrounded by people, it was like they were completely alone.

"Jess." His voice was soft, and the look in his eyes made her breath catch. "I'll stay, if you want me to."

"Stay?" The word trembled out. She wouldn't even let herself consider what it might mean.

"In Los Angeles."

Oh. He did mean that.

Jess took a sip of cocoa she carried to give herself time to sort out her thoughts. He'd put the ball in her court. While she couldn't deny there was a spark between them, the fear that he'd leave as soon as the next gig popped up was too strong. What if she said yes and he left anyway? It would break her.

She needed to buy some time.

"New Year's Eve," she said, lowering the cup and meeting his eyes. "At midnight. If I kiss you…" *It means you convinced me. That I want you to stay.* She couldn't bring herself to say the words.

"If you kiss me, I'll stay," he clarified. "And if you don't…then I'll know where we stand."

"Yes." All of this had started with a kiss at midnight. It seemed right to bring it full circle, no matter how it turned out.

Nik nodded. "It's a date."

After they finished their drinks, Nik walked her to her car in the garage.

"Did you have fun?"

"Maybe I did," she replied with a coy smile. She couldn't lie and say she hadn't, but it was still too soon to give him the upper hand.

When he passed her the bag containing her new lipstick and the gifts she'd purchased for Naomi and her agent, their hands brushed. The barest contact, but it pulled at her and made her want more.

He stood close, looking down at her with brown eyes gone soft and dreamy. Was he going to kiss her? Her breath hitched in anticipation of the touch of his lips. A beat passed, and when he didn't lean in, she realized he was waiting for her to make the first move.

Jess didn't consider herself shy, but something made her want to take things slow. Instead of a kiss, she reached up to give him a hug. It had been an excellent date, and he deserved that much, at least.

And also? She just wanted to.

She shut her eyes for a second to savor the feel of his hard, capable body surrounding her, to breathe in the subtle scent of his cologne—something woodsy with notes of amber that made her think of the color of his eyes.

Because she wanted to hold on, she let go. "You have my number," she said, opening the car door. "Keep me posted about date number two." *In other words, the ball's back in your court, buddy.*

"I will." The words rang with a note of promise.

She hoped he did. Not because she fully believed in him or this holiday magic business. But she'd had fun, and yeah, she wanted to see him again.

Hopefully her heart's defenses were strong enough to withstand whatever else he had in store for them.

———

Nik walked into his brother's house to find Natasha sitting at the kitchen counter, working on her laptop.

She looked up when Nik stopped in the arched doorway, blinking at him through red-framed glasses. "Hey. Were you out with Jess?"

"Yeah." He'd already told Tash about the three dates thing. He pulled out a chair and sat across from her. "How well do you know her?" he asked, then quickly added, "Not that I'm digging for info or anything. Just curious."

Natasha frowned at the ceiling. "Not super well, come to think of it. She's newer to the cast, a bit younger. I haven't really hung out with her outside of work or group settings. How was your date?"

"Good." He shifted in the chair, trying to get comfortable. "I mean, I think it was good. She's still on board for the second date, so I guess she had a nice time."

He couldn't figure Jess out. Sometimes it seemed like she really liked him, but then she'd switch on a dime, and he could tell she was holding back. Was it that she didn't trust him? She'd warmed up as the night went on, and he hadn't mistaken her genuine enjoyment when they'd danced. Swing dancing for a crowd of dozens of onlookers hadn't been part of his plan, but dating, like dancing, sometimes required improvisation.

He hadn't planned on telling her he'd stay, either, but with the snow and cocoa and everything, it had just slipped out. He meant it, but it was clear Jess didn't believe that yet.

"Having never been on a date with you, I couldn't say," Natasha was saying. "But if you were your usual charming self, I don't see how she could resist you."

Dimitri walked in then. "What are you saying? I'm not charming?"

Tash grinned at him. "You can be, but I think we both know Nik has you beat in that department."

"As long as it's not in any other departments." He took her hand and pulled her into his arms. "Besides, you don't like charming guys."

She let out an exaggerated sigh. "You're right. I don't. I like moody grouches."

She was laughing when Dimitri lowered his head to kiss her.

Nik slipped out of the kitchen to give them some privacy and headed to his room. Or, rather, the guest room. Same space, different distinction.

This wasn't his home anymore.

When he'd sold his car and moved all his stuff into storage earlier in the year, it was with the intention of being even more free and detached than he already was.

Now? He just felt unmoored, like a rowboat stuck in the middle of a lake.

He recalled the conversation he'd had with Jess nearly a year ago. At the time, the thought of being settled had scared him. As a performer, complacency felt like giving up, and their talk had likely contributed to his decision to move out of his brother's house. But watching Mitya and Tash grow closer made Nik take a good, hard look at his own life, and his place in the Kovalenko family.

The role wasn't always comfortable, but he'd been the little brother for a long time. Now, it looked like he'd be a brother-in-law soon. His cousin Alex's baby would be born in a few months; maybe Tash and Mitya would have babies too. He hoped they did. He was looking forward to being an uncle and planned to spoil the heck out of his nieces and nephews.

But what did he want for himself? What new space did he want to claim within the family dynamic? He'd been very small when their family immigrated to America, and he'd had an easier time adapting than Dimitri had. Plus, he'd always had Mitya looking out for him. Part of his reason for taking touring gigs had been to break away from that, to carve out his own niche independent of his famous older brother.

And he'd done it. He'd performed on Broadway, at the West End, as a backup dancer for multi-platinum pop stars—hell, he'd even danced during a Super Bowl halftime show.

He'd made a name for himself in this industry. He'd seen the world. He'd spent years searching for an elusive sense of fulfillment and purpose, and come up empty-handed.

But when he'd seen Jess at that party, standing across the room in a cute Christmas shirt, it was like something shifted inside him, as if the missing piece he'd been looking for had magically appeared, right where it belonged.

What the hell did it all mean?

All he knew was he had a few local opportunities on the table —thanks to his kickass agent—no home to call his own, and a woman who didn't believe he was willing to stay if she only gave him the word.

In other words…not much.

He was too worn out to contemplate such heavy thoughts any

further. After changing into basketball shorts, he headed for Mitya's home gym. Maybe sweating would help shut his brain off. This endeavor with Jess had to work. It had to. If it didn't... well, he'd cross that bridge when he came to it. For now, he had a second date to plan.

Chapter Four

December 19th

J ess woke to a slew of text messages, and her social media mentions had exploded overnight. Sure enough, the video of her dance with Nik had gone viral, and everyone had seen it.

She squinted at her phone as she brewed a cup of coffee. Most of the texts were from Naomi, but Rhianne's name was in there, too, along with messages from her mom and her sister. Fuckin' fantastic. Those could wait.

There was only one text from Rhianne and eight from Naomi, so she checked Rhianne's first.

God, she was never going to be able to look at Rhianne the same way after that Rudolph boob thing.

Rhianne: *Saw the video. Omg. Were you on a date with Nik? Did you KISS again? Are you with him now? Tell me everything.*

Jess groaned and set the phone down on the counter. A hit of caffeine was in order before she could read the rest, which would undoubtedly be worse. She doctored her coffee with a heavy pour of almond milk to cool it down and a dash of stevia for sweetness, guzzled half, then picked up her phone again. She checked Naomi's first, not yet ready to see what her family had to say.

Naomi: *YOOOOOOO*

Naomi: *THAT VIDEOOOOOO*

Naomi: ::three screaming face emojis, three heart-eyes emojis::

Naomi: *Are you going out with him???*

Naomi: *Also you guys are amazing dancers, that goes without saying.*

Naomi: *It was SO CUTE*

Naomi: *But like*

Naomi: *What does it meeeeeean??*

Naomi never said in one text what she could say in twenty, and with approximately ten times the correct number of vowels.

Jess wished she had an answer for the last question. Clearly Nik liked her, but how much?

I'll stay, if you want me to.

She wanted to believe him, she really did, but her track record —and his, for that matter—did not support his statement.

Another text came through from her mom, so she checked those next.

Mommy: *Hi baby! I saw your video on TV!*

Mommy: *You looked so beautiful, Jessie.*

Mommy: *Daddy and I hope you can come visit soon!*

Jess shut her eyes against the subtle guilt trip. What her mother didn't realize was that being home was incredibly stressful for her. Her parents had fought constantly when she was a kid, her dad even going so far as to leave for long stretches at a time. But now that she and Jaina had moved out and it was just the two of them? They were inseparable! *What the fuck, guys,* she wanted to say to them. *You couldn't have sorted out your shit earlier so you didn't pass that baggage on to your kids?*

So no, she didn't visit as often as she could, or should, but she still visited more than she wanted to. And if deep down she still worried that her presence would ruin their relationship again, well, who could blame her?

She checked Jaina's text last.

Jaina: *Sis! What's up with you and that hottie in the video? You got something going on there?* ::winky face emoji, eggplant emoji::

Jaina used that damned eggplant emoji more than anyone else Jess knew.

Before her eyes, texts from Joel Clarke—one of the other pros on *The Dance Off*—and two of her friends from rooftop yoga appeared. She didn't even dare check her social media notifications.

Everybody wanted to know what was up with her and Nik. And he seemed to be the only person in her life who hadn't reached out this morning.

Since she didn't have an answer for any of them, she put the phone down again without looking at the new messages. A second later, it buzzed with an incoming call.

She snatched it up, half-expecting to see Nik's face on the screen. She'd already attached one of their dumb—but actually super cute—Christmas selfies from the night before to his number. But it wasn't Nik. It was her agent, Lorena Malcolm.

"Lorena? What's up?"

Lorena got right to the point. "I'm not going to ask you what's going on with Nik Kovalenko because that's your personal business, and you know I don't get involved in that—unless of course you *want* to tell me, in which case I'm all ears—but the video of you two swing dancing at the Americana went viral overnight, and your professional life *is* my business. I'm calling to tell you to hurry up and get dressed because you have three—at least three, for now—talk show appearances lined up for today. This is *great* exposure for you and I'm already getting inquiries about other gigs."

Jess blinked, taking a second to sort all that out. Lorena was a middle-aged Italian woman from Long Island, and she talked a mile a fucking minute. Since Jess didn't want to discuss Nik with her agent, she chose to focus on the most pressing issue. "When is the first show?"

"In an hour! You've gotta get moving, sweetie. They'll do hair and makeup for you."

Jess hurried into her bedroom. "They have someone on staff who can do my hair?"

"Yes, I already asked."

"What should I wear?" She tore through her closet, shoving hangers aside to reach the fancier garments hidden in the back.

"Blouse, nice jeans, and high heels should do the job. Wear that green and gold statement necklace. Don't suppose you've got any Christmas-themed shirts?"

Jess shuddered. "Hell no."

"Worth a shot. I'll meet you there with some poinsettia earrings my kids got me a billion years ago. Wear a shirt that'll match. And bring shoes you can swing dance in, just in case."

Poinsettia earrings. What was she getting herself into? But this was why Lorena was such a good agent—she thought of everything. Jess thanked her and disconnected. Then she took the fastest shower ever, grabbed the hangers with her on-screen outfit and the bag with her shoes, and ran out the door in yoga clothes and sneakers.

She hoped Lorena was right about this video giving her career a boost. Since she had a pretty good deal at *The Dance Off*, she hadn't been auditioning much, and this might send some new opportunities her way.

If only she had some idea of what she wanted those to be. She loved competitive ballroom dance, and getting to do it on the biggest stage possible—*The Dance Off* literally had *millions* of viewers—was great, but she wouldn't mind taking on something a little more...fulfilling.

If she'd had a second to think since waking up, she might have guessed that Nik would *also* be called in for the morning show. But she hadn't had a second, and she hadn't guessed that he'd be there. So when she walked into the makeup room at *LA Morning with Flip and Rashida* to find Nik in one of the makeup chairs, she stopped short. A guy with the sharpest eyebrows she'd ever seen was combing Nik's curls into a smooth, stylish 'do.

"You're here," she blurted out. Damn, she needed more caffeine.

Nik looked up from his phone and sent her a thousand-watt grin, like he was overjoyed to see her. "Of course. Been waiting for you." He gestured at the counter, which was covered in trays of makeup. A lone to-go cup sat amidst the eyeshadow palettes. "Got you a coffee. Had them put almond milk in it since that's what you requested yesterday with the hot chocolate."

Still half asleep, she had no defenses against his sweetness. She slumped into the chair next to him and mumbled a thank you.

What does it mean? Naomi had asked, albeit with an excessive number of vowels. The talk show hosts were likely to ask the same. God, what was she doing here? She didn't have an answer for any of them. She just didn't fucking know. There was nothing to tell, right? He was her former coworker's brother. They'd hung out together one time. No big deal. Easy-peasy.

The Nik Kovalenko she'd been checking up on—okay, fine, stalking—on social media on and off during the year had been in line with the Nik who'd kissed her in the kitchen on New Year's Eve. He wanted adventure. He wanted to see the world. He didn't want to be tied down. His Instagram and Snapchat showed clips and stills of a life in motion. In every shot, he was in a new place, often with new people. He was doing cool things, having those adventures he'd spoken of. Bungee jumping, cliff diving, skiing, riding a motorcycle, eating snails, posing with fans at stage doors in cities all over the world. The hashtag #lovemylife was prevalent. That Nik didn't want to be tied down.

She couldn't help but focus on the disconnect between the person in those pictures and the one who sat next to her, smiling. The one who'd thought to bring her coffee with her preferred choice of non-dairy milk substitute.

It was the most romantic fucking thing she could imagine.

Lorena bustled into the makeup room then, saving Jess from

the awkwardness of having to rehash the date with Nik. "I've got the earrings!" she trilled.

Oh, joy.

"SO, ARE YOU GUYS DATING?"

The talk show co-host—Elena—had an expectant, almost maniacal gleam in her eyes, identical to the hosts Nik had been interviewed by earlier in the day. Hungry for news, for a scoop. As much as he wanted to know the answer to that question, too, he had no interest in fueling the gossip mill. And by now, he and Jess had their answer down pat.

"We're just friends," Jess was quick to reply, dismissing the rumor with an almost negligent hand wave. "Besides, Nik doesn't even live in Los Angeles."

Nik just smiled through it. When the interview turned to their personal holiday traditions, that was his cue to take over.

"We love the winter holidays in my family," he began, to the delight of the host. "My family celebrates Christmas on both December 25th and on January 7th, according to the Eastern Orthodox calendar, and the extended family on my father's side celebrates Hanukkah."

The other host—Giovanni—introduced the next segment. "Now we're going to have Nik and Jess tell us a little about the dance style in their viral video and show us some moves."

Nik, Jess, and the two hosts got up from their chairs and moved to a clear section of the stage.

"Now, what's the dance called?" Elena asked, even though she knew perfectly well since it was written in her notes.

"The Lindy hop," Jess answered.

Giovanni jumped in. "And that's a type of swing dance?" Again, it was in his notes. This was part of the game.

Nik's turn. "If you go to a studio to learn swing dance, there are three main types they'll probably teach: East Coast Swing, West Coast Swing, and Lindy hop."

They'd done this enough times now that Jess picked up the thread of explanation right on cue.

"The Lindy hop, as a dance style, originated in Harlem at the Savoy Ballroom in 1928," Jess explained. "It's a fusion dance that evolved over time with jazz music, and it's known for its basic step, the swing out."

Every time she talked about it, her demeanor brightened. With her eyes shining and her dimple flashing, she was a joy to watch. Nik hoped his open admiration wasn't clear on his face, but if it was, well...so be it.

"And that's what we're going to learn today?" Giovanni asked, and Jess nodded.

Nik paired up with Elena, a petite woman with a sleek red bob and too much bronzer. "This is the hold," he said for the cameras. "I hold Elena's right hand lightly with my left—no thumbs."

"Oh, sorry." Elena giggled and blushed under the makeup.

He smiled to put her at ease. "No worries. This is a learning environment."

A few feet away, Jess did the same with Giovanni. "I put my left hand on Giovanni's arm, just below his shoulder, and he should put his right hand on my left shoulder blade." When Giovanni didn't move, she gave him an encouraging nod. "Come on, man. Do it."

"Whoops." Giovanni laughed and completed the hold. "I got caught up in the explanation."

Nik explained the eight-count pattern, and Jess gave instructions on the stance. Once they'd guided the hosts through the swing out steps a few times to music, Elena and Giovanni moved aside to let Nik and Jess take center stage.

Jess stepped close to Nik and got in hold.

"Ready?" he asked.

Her eyes held a glint of humor. "Always."

The song's bassline started, and they flew into the dance.

This, by far, was Nik's favorite part of the whole media circus—getting to dance with Jess again, to hold her in his arms without anyone wondering what it meant, and just letting the music carry them away.

They'd put together a short, fast routine backstage before the first interview of the day, dancing to a recent electro-funk pop hit they'd been able to quickly get permission to use. The objective was to go full out, as fast as they could, no holding back. So, even though Jess was the one doing most of the jumps, that meant Nik had to put in equal energy to balance her.

Starting with a swing out, they shook it up with swivels, kick steps, and spins. Their spirited intensity matched the bubbly vocals and bouncy beat, and at each turn, they found the camera with grins and winks. The vibe was flirtatious, a courtship between him, Jess, and the viewers.

When the heavy horn section kicked in, they shifted into the bigger tricks. Nik always took dance seriously, but especially when he was dancing with a partner. The moves could be dangerous if he didn't stay focused, attuned to Jess's energy and his own strength.

First a push out, where Jess used the tension of their joined hands to leap at him. Nik caught her hip and pushed her back out, admiring the force of her jump. When she landed, they circled each other with a series of deep swivels, throwing their knees side to side and showing off for the audience. Jess even stuck her tongue out at him as she improvised with a twirl.

A vision floated through Nik's mind, of pulling Jess close for the next move and planting a kiss right on that sarcastic mouth. It would interrupt the dance, but her sexy little smiles and flirty winks were driving him wild with need. But he filed it away for later. If he had anything to do with it, they'd have more opportunities to dance together in the future. Without an audience.

Catching her hand again, they launched into a Frankie pop, jumping away from each other on one foot, coming back together with a small hop, and then rotating in the air—with Jess doing a full three-hundred-and-sixty-degree spin before landing again.

The studio audience murmured in awe, then cheered as Nik and Jess swung out into their last move.

The flash of pleasure in Jess's eyes probably matched his own. There was nothing like dancing in front of a live audience. As professional dancers, they spent every moment practicing, but still, anything could go wrong. So when things went right? There was a rush of satisfaction, even after all this time.

And the crowd was going to love the next move.

The Kaye Dip wasn't a particularly sexy finish, but there was body contact, and ending in a dip was always a crowd pleaser. Besides, he'd take any excuse to hold Jess in his arms.

Nik stepped his leg around Jess, popped her up onto his back, then swung her legs outward, bringing her to rest on his opposite hip in their ending pose. The music faded, and the hosts rushed them, clapping and gushing praise.

Nik swung Jess out from the aerial, and after she was steady on her feet, he released her hand, even though all he wanted to do was hold on. She turned away to smile and wave for the camera, and he reminded himself to be patient. After all, he still had two more dates with her.

The show broke for commercial, and they were ushered backstage while the next activity was set up.

"In the next segment, you're going to decorate wreaths with the hosts," a production assistant explained as the makeup crew hurried over to pat the sweat off their faces and reapply powder. "Any pine allergies?"

Jess balked. "Any what?"

"We're fine," Nik assured the PA.

When they were alone, she muttered, "I didn't realize pine allergies were a thing. I'm so using that next year to get out of doing this kind of shit. From now on, yes, I do have pine allergies."

He laughed, and it took everything in him not to hug her right then. Holding her while they danced had been wonderful, but it wasn't enough.

Jess's agent, Lorena, bustled over then. She was five feet if she was an inch, and carried a shoulder bag approximately the size of a small car.

"Jess, honey, I have some great news." Lorena brandished her phone, but the screen was off. "I just got a call from the Heartflix Channel—you know, the ones who make all those romantic holiday movies?"

Nik had a feeling he knew where this was going. He smothered a smile as Jess rolled her eyes.

"I've heard of them," she said. "But I definitely don't watch those movies."

Lorena waved that away with a flick of her hand. "They saw the video of you two dancing in the mall and they think you're *perfect* for a guest spot in one of the movies they have coming out next year. They're even willing to fit you in before the next season of *The Dance Off* starts."

Jess's eyes went wide with horror. "Wait, they want me to be in one of their *Christmas* movies?"

Nik turned his laugh into a cough. When Jess glared at him, he schooled his features into an expression of solemnity. *No laughing over here.*

Lowering her voice, Jess leaned in toward her agent. "Lorena, you know I hate Christmas. And those movies are just dripping with overblown sentimentality."

"Those movies get millions of viewers and repeat airings," Lorena pointed out. "And there's a lot of overlap between their viewers and people who watch—and vote for—*The Dance Off*."

Jess pursed her lips like she wanted to argue, but couldn't.

Lorena gave her a motherly pat on the arm. "Just think about it, okay? And then say yes. Ciao!"

She scurried off, leaving them in a cloud of gardenia-scented perfume.

"Don't laugh," Jess grumbled.

"I wouldn't dream of it." Nik pressed his lips together hard to hold back a chuckle.

A PA hurried over to collect them, and after the wreaths were made—and they'd washed pine sap off their hands—they took photos with the crew, filmed a couple segments for the show's social media channels, and rushed off to the next interview.

And then it was more of the same.

"So, are you two dating?"

"Show us some dance moves!"

"What are your personal holiday traditions?"

During those moments, when Nik talked about his family, it seemed like Jess was watching him intently, as if she were soaking in these details about his life.

God, he hoped so. He was already falling for her, and she'd be a tough nut to crack. But, like the Nutcracker, he would... No, that was a bad analogy. He knew the story too well, having danced it multiple times in his career—it was a boring gig, but paid well. Regardless, he was determined to bring this woman some Christmas cheer, like the Sugar Plum Fairy and her band of merry makers in the Land of Sweets.

Just like that, he knew what their second date would be.

———

AFTER THEIR LAST INTERVIEW, Jess wanted nothing more than to go home and put on her pajamas. The day had been a whirlwind of invasive questions, repetitive dance instruction, and a lot of waiting around in green rooms. And Lorena hadn't been kidding —in addition to the Heartflix offer, three TV sitcoms and a soap opera had reached out to inquire about guest spots. Jess knew she should be thrilled, but everything was happening so fast, it made her head spin.

Nik caught up to her as she was entering the elevator. She wouldn't tell him so, but it had been nice having him with her. This was her first time doing the talk show circuit without the entire cast of *The Dance Off* along for the ride, and it would have been overwhelming without Nik's steady, soothing presence at her side.

When the doors swished behind them, he leaned against the side of the elevator car with his hands in his pockets and gazed down on her with a small smile on that sexy mouth of his. "Come over to Dimitri's tomorrow," he said, voice low. "I have our second date planned."

Since his smooth rumble and A+ leaning skills were making her all fluttery inside, she tried to keep her tone teasing. "You mean today wasn't our second date?"

He chuckled. "Today definitely doesn't count. I had to spend the whole day trying to pretend I wasn't into you. And we were dancing. Today was work."

Riding high on the media stops and believing her own hype about how there wasn't anything serious between them, she flirted more. "Technically we danced yesterday, too. Was that *work*?"

"If yesterday didn't count, that means I have three more dates with you."

She poked a finger into his chest. "Nuh-uh, dude. You have two. No wishing for more wishes."

"Okay, fine. Two. But today didn't count, and you'll come to my place tomorrow. Deal?"

"You live to make deals, don't you? Fine. You got it. What should I wear?"

"Something you don't mind getting a little messy."

"Messy?" Her mind supplied all sorts of messy things they could do together. "What kinda kinky shit do you have planned?"

He laughed, low and husky, and the sound tickled along her skin like the brush of a feather. The elevator doors opened, and they headed for the building exit together.

"It's actually so wholesome, you're going to laugh when you find out."

"Hmm, I don't know if wholesome is my jam."

"Trust me. Come over at noon. And bring a bathing suit."

"Excuse me? What were you just saying about wholesome?"

"It's gonna be hot, and we have a pool. Just in case."

She wasn't buying his "wholesome" nonsense for a minute, but she'd pack a bathing suit anyway. Just in case. Dimitri's pool *was* really nice. And he had a hot tub, too.

Maybe things would get a little kinky after all.

By the time Jess was back in her apartment, she had fifteen texts from Naomi. The last one read: *Let me know when you get home. I'm coming over with margarita mix.*

She typed back, *I'm home. Drinks needed. And can you braid my hair?*

When Naomi arrived, Jess opened the door clad in a shiny gold string bikini.

Naomi's brown eyes went wide. "Whoa, what kind of party is this? I think I'm overdressed."

Jess ushered her inside. "I'm going to Nik's house tomorrow for our second date and he told me to bring a swimsuit. His brother has a pool and a hot tub."

Bustling into the kitchen with her grocery bags clinking, Naomi shot Jess an accusatory look over her shoulder. "Second date? You didn't even tell me about the first one!"

"I know, I know." Jess fiddled with the straps on her top as Naomi unloaded bottles onto the kitchen counter. Two types of tequila, two types of margarita mix, and a bottle of seltzer. From a second bag she produced chips, cut veggies, salsa, guacamole, and margarita salt.

Once the bags were empty, she turned to Jess and waved a hand expectantly. "And?"

"We just went shopping at the mall. And then we danced—but you saw that part."

"So, it *was* a date. Ice?"

Jess opened the freezer and pulled out an ice tray.

While Naomi mixed the drinks, Jess put the snacks on serving dishes and told her about the three holiday-themed dates. She hadn't mentioned them at Rhianne's party because she wanted to see how the first date went.

"So, that's why you're in a bikini."

Jess glanced at herself. She'd almost forgotten she was mostly naked, drinking margaritas in her kitchen. "Yeah, basically. I need you to help me pick one out, and then braid my hair in case I go in the pool."

"Let's see what you've got."

They took the margaritas into Jess's bedroom, where she had upended the swimsuit bin from her closet onto the queen-sized bed.

"Damn, girl, you got a lot of bikinis!"

"We all have our vices." Jess sifted through the scraps of spandex. "I want to find one that says 'sexy' without also saying 'obvious,' you know?"

"If that's the case, what you're wearing now is pretty obvious."

Jess glanced down at herself again. "I guess you're right."

Naomi plucked a shimmering green top with a mermaid scale pattern from the pile. "How about this?"

"No, that's one I took to Brazil for Carnaval. It doesn't even cover my ass."

"Ah. So it goes in the obvious pile."

They continued to sort and debate the merits of Jess's swimsuit collection. The decidedly unsexy one-pieces Jess wore for swimming laps at the gym were also out.

"What about this?"

Jess cocked her head, considering the white one-piece Naomi held up. It had bits of netting and artful cutouts that made it sexy and stylish. "I'll try it on."

When she emerged from the master bathroom wearing the white suit, Naomi raised her margarita glass. "That's the one, my dear."

"Excellent." Jess did a little shimmy, then clinked her glass to Naomi's.

After changing into sweats, Jess shoved all the bathing suits into their bin while Naomi sat on the edge of the bed.

"I feel like a proud mama," Naomi said, pretending to wipe away tears. "Baby's first hot tub date."

Jess rolled her eyes. "I know I work for a reality show, but there will be no cameras on this date."

"How do you know? There were cameras on the first one."

"That was spontaneous!"

"Are you sure?" Naomi raised a brow.

Jess paused, then shook her head. "Nik wouldn't do that."

Sure, she still had doubts about his wanderlust sending him packing again, but he wouldn't use her for a publicity stunt. Of that, at least, she was certain.

"How do you know?"

"I know." Jess snapped the lid back on the bin. "He's…a good person."

"I'm just looking out for you. You dated some real losers when you first moved here."

With a sigh, Jess shoved the bin back into her closet. "Yes, I remember. Come on, those chips aren't going to eat themselves, and I need you to braid my hair."

That night, after Naomi left, Jess thought back, not to her friend's suggestion that Nik was using her in some way—that just didn't gel with what she'd seen of him at all—but to one of Naomi's text messages from that morning.

What does it mean?

She puzzled over it as she packed her bag for the next day, tossing in the white bathing suit, a clarifying shampoo, and her new Holly Jolly Berry lipstick.

Maybe she didn't have to know what it all meant. Maybe she could just live in the moment and enjoy spending time with this man. Wasn't that enough?

It would have to be. Because as much as she was starting to trust him, she still didn't believe he'd stick around.

Chapter Five

December 20th

J ess entered Dimitri's house and was greeted with the scents
of gingerbread, chocolate, and cinnamon. Jazzy versions of
Christmas carols played softly in the background.

"*Cookies?*" She turned to Nik in accusation and surprise. "This
is your messy activity?"

"Yeah. Baking holiday cookies is tradition."

"Boy, you weren't kidding about wholesome."

He quirked an eyebrow. "Why, what were you expecting?"

She hunched her shoulders, recalling the steamy images that
had kept her up last night involving champagne, honey, and
whipped cream. "Don't worry about it."

"Come say hi to everyone," Nik said, guiding her toward the
kitchen, where the mouthwatering aromas originated.

Everyone? They weren't going to be alone for this date, either?
Maybe this was a double date with Dimitri and Natasha. That
would make sense, since Dimitri *was* Nik's brother and this *was*
his house.

Still, Jess felt a vague sense of disappointment. She'd meant what she said about not being Nik's girl in this port, but it would've been nice to spend some time alone with him. As reluctant as she was to put all her trust in him, he was still a lot of fun to hang out with.

Okay, and maybe she'd be all right with messing around a little. Nik was super hot.

Nik stopped in the kitchen doorway and ushered her in. "I believe you know everyone here," he said.

When Jess entered the room, shock mixed with delight. It wasn't just Dimitri and Natasha in the kitchen.

"Gina!"

"Hey, girl!" Gina, another one of Jess's former coworkers on *The Dance Off*, set down a handful of frosting tubes on the counter.

Gina hurried over to give Jess a hug and a kiss on the cheek. "Good to see you. You remember Stone." She gestured to her giant of a boyfriend, who'd been Gina's celebrity partner on *The Dance Off* earlier that year.

"Hi, Stone." Jess sent him a wave. Apparently this was a *triple* date. "I didn't know you guys were in town."

Jess hadn't hung out a ton with Gina and Natasha—she was closer to Rhianne, Mila, and Joel—but she liked them just fine.

"Just a short visit," Gina said. "Tash and I always used to do the tree and cookie stuff together, and we didn't want to skip it this year. I'm glad you can join us."

"Me, too," Jess said, shooting a look over her shoulder at Nik, who loitered by the arched doorway with a smug grin. There was no way she could get away with being a Scrooge around the others.

Nik joined her at the counter, and while he didn't touch her, Jess was fully aware of his body all the same. It was like he emitted some kind of sexy force field only she could feel and that was impossible to ignore.

"Did you guys get those in Alaska?" Nik asked, gesturing at Stone and Gina's tops.

It was then that Jess noticed they wore matching Christmas

sweaters—Gina's was red, Stone's was green, and they both had moose silhouettes on them.

Wait a minute.

Upon closer inspection, Gina's had not just one moose, but *two* moose. Mooses? No, the plural of moose was moose. Either way, these moose were getting it on, moose-style, right across Gina's chest.

Well, now she *had* to know what Stone's moose was doing. Jess moved closer, squinting. The moose was…

Pooping. The moose was pooping.

Stone let out a long-suffering sigh, but Gina flashed a wide grin. "You wouldn't believe all the bizarre moose merchandise they have in Alaska," she said. "They're on *everything*. You guys want moose undies? I can get you some next time we visit Stone's family."

When she went to arrange the cookie cutters next to the rolling pin, Stone leaned down from his great height and muttered, "Trust me, you don't want them."

Jess turned to Nik after Stone had gone back to setting out containers of cookie decorations. "Well, now I'm just curious," she whispered.

"I know," Nik replied under his breath. "How bad could they be?"

She sent him a sly smile. "I bet you'd look cute in moose undies."

"Excuse me." He sounded offended, but his amber brown eyes turned molten and his voice dropped to a sensuous purr. "I look cute in *anything*."

Or nothing, Jess thought. Yeah, she'd bet he looked real good in nothing at all.

With that delicious image in her head, she got to work helping the others set up.

———

Nik was relieved when Jess fell into an easy conversation with Gina and Tash. She'd seemed apprehensive when he'd told her about the others, and he'd worried the whole idea for this date had been a mistake.

But they'd agreed to three holiday-themed dates, and for him, a huge part of the holidays was spending time with friends and family. And these people fell into that category.

Dimitri, of course, was his brother, and Natasha was near enough to being family at this point. And while Gina was Tash's best friend, Nik had never expected Stone and Dimitri to get along so well. They were both so different: Stone the very definition of "outdoorsy," and Dimitri the cosmopolitan restaurateur. But they got on famously somehow, bonding over stuff like home repair projects and beard maintenance.

Nik liked Stone, too. Dude was fun, and he had some kickass stories about living in Alaska. Nik hadn't been there yet, but he wanted to go. Gina had recommended he visit during summer instead of winter.

Nik couldn't think of a better way to spend the day than hanging out with these four, with Jess at his side.

Well, maybe he could think of a few other things he and Jess could do, but he wouldn't rush her.

One date left.

As much as the previous day's media visits had worn on him, he'd enjoyed getting to spend extra time with Jess. In hindsight, three dates didn't seem like enough.

More and more, he was sure she was the missing piece he'd been searching for. Her quick wit and dry humor belied a sweetness and sensitivity that made him want to gather her in his arms and show her that her heart would be safe with him. When he was with her, the restless feeling that had propelled him through years of touring gigs finally quieted. For once, he felt like he could be still.

A year ago, these impulses would've scared him. Now, he just wanted to take his time getting to know her better and proving to her how good they could be.

While the others worked on the cookies, Nik took Jess into the living room to start on the tree—and to get her alone. The scent of gingerbread followed them.

"You don't bake?" she asked.

"I can follow a recipe, but it's better if my brother and I don't cook or bake at the same time. We both recall 'what Mama said' differently. Besides, I love decorating Christmas trees."

She eyed the bare tree standing in the living room. "Aren't they a fire hazard?"

He laughed. "Only if you don't water them. And anyway, this tree is fake. Dimitri doesn't like getting pine needles all over his house."

Jess put her hands on her hips. "If it's a fake tree, does it even count?"

"Oh, look who's the authority on Christmas authenticity all of a sudden."

"I'm just saying, if you're not getting that pine smell, what's the point?"

"We've got that covered." He pointed to the wall, where a scented plug-in gave off a rich, piney odor.

"Ah, so that's where the smell was coming from."

Nik opened two big plastic tubs filled to the brim with lights, garland, baubles, stockings, and more. "Dimitri likes the tree to have a 'theme,' which he rotates year to year. This time it's silver and dark blue."

"Your brother seems like a guy who likes what he likes."

Nik coughed out a laugh. "You have no idea. I've celebrated Christmas with him every year of my life. But it's different at home. Our mom gets a real tree, and there's no theme. When we were kids, we used to make our own ornaments, and she's kept them all these years."

"That sounds nice." Jess fingered a length of blue ribbon. "We didn't even put up a tree every year."

Sadness tinged her voice, and despite his earlier resolve to let Jess open up on her own, Nik couldn't stop from asking, "Why not?"

Jess examined the beaded detail on a silver star ornament. "Let's just say the holidays weren't usually a happy time."

Nik gave in to the urge to touch her, smoothing his hand up and down her arm in a soothing gesture. "I shouldn't have pressed."

"No, it's okay that you did." She gave him a small smile and moved closer. "Besides, I said 'usually.' This holiday season is turning out to be pretty fun."

When she laced her fingers through his and tilted her chin up, Nik took the hint. Bending his head, he pressed his lips to hers in a soft, sweet kiss. The scent of cherries blended into all the holiday smells around them, like it was the only thing that had been missing and now the experience was complete.

The moment stretched, wrapping him in a comforting easiness he'd never felt before.

So, this was what it was like to feel settled.

He could have taken the kiss deeper, but with the smell of cookies, the tinkling piano rendition of "I'll Be Home for Christmas," and Jess's emotional admission, it felt right to keep the touch of their mouths soft and languid, an almost innocent exploring of lips.

Nik lifted his head, and for a second, they just smiled at each other. Then Jess gave his hand a squeeze. "Come on," she said. "This tree isn't going to trim itself."

They worked well together, untangling the lights someone— probably Dimitri—had been too impatient to store properly the year before. Jess looped enormous sparkly baubles over her ears so they hung like earrings, then hammed it up, winking and blowing kisses at Nik through his phone's camera. Laughing, she wrapped him in silver garland, then made him pose with her for selfies.

"These are too good," she said, skimming through the pics on her phone. "We should post one."

He peeked over her shoulder as she scrolled, then stopped her. "That one."

It was a close up shot of the two of them caught mid-laughter, mouths wide open, eyes crinkling as they looked at each other. The half-trimmed tree was blurry, but still visible behind them.

Jess hesitated for a moment, then nodded. "Okay."

She added a bunch of emojis in the caption, including the Christmas tree and chocolate chip cookie, then clicked "post."

People were going to read into it. The talk show hosts who'd peppered them with "Are you dating?" questions might even latch onto it as proof that they were.

But it didn't matter what any of them thought. Jess was the only person whose opinion meant anything to Nik right now.

They'd just finished transferring the garland from his body to the tree when Gina stuck her head into the living room. "The first batches are cool enough to decorate," she called, then disappeared.

"Ready to join the others?" he asked, not wanting to push Jess into being more social than she wanted to be.

"Yes." She sniffed the air. "Smells good."

Nik cleared his throat. "You have, uh, a little something…" He gestured at his ears. When Jess touched her own ear, she burst out laughing. She still wore the Christmas baubles.

"Let's put those back where they belong," she said, removing the loops from her ear and hanging them on the tree instead. Then she slipped her hand into his as they walked to the kitchen.

Nik got that easy, settled feeling again. Why had he spent so long running from this? It was the best feeling in the world.

Inside the kitchen, the counter was covered with racks of sugar and gingerbread cookies in various shapes—people, yes, but also stars, unicorns, and…moose.

While Dimitri and Natasha worked on prepping the next batch to bake, Jess and Nik sat at the counter with Gina and Stone to decorate.

"I didn't realize unicorns had to do with Yuletide cheer," Jess said, picking up one of the cookies.

"Unicorns are very festive." Nik chose a sugar cookie person. "Didn't you know they're second cousins to reindeer?"

She snickered. "I must have missed that day in biology class."

It very soon became clear why they were dancers instead of artists. Dimitri, disgusted with their attempts at making gingerbread people—and animals—threw aside his apron and took over. Nik remembered all the times they'd sat at the kitchen table decorating cookies and Christmas ornaments with their parents. Even when they were kids, Dimitri had always shown artistic ability.

Gina and Natasha commandeered the oven. There was a lot of giggling over the cookie trays, and the next batch that came out of the oven looked distinctly like...

Dimitri stared at the cookies, horrified. "Are those *dicks?*"

Stone, who'd been putting the star on the Christmas tree because he was tallest one present by far, happened to walk back into the kitchen at that exact moment. He took one glance at the cookies and shot Gina an exasperated look. "Was this your idea?"

Her response was to dissolve into giggles.

Jess elbowed Nik in his side. "What do those represent?" she asked from the corner of her mouth. "The ghost of Christmas penis?"

Nik doubled over, and Dimitri and Stone hastily took over the rest of the baking. Jess joined the other women in decorating the Christmas Cocks, as the cookies had been dubbed, and since Nik knew it would amuse her, he ate one. Jess's delighted peal of laughter was well worth his brother's eye roll.

"Look, Macho," Natasha called out to Dimitri, holding up one of her cookies. "We used the little sugar pearl things as jizz."

"Mine has red and green pubes," Gina added. "'Tis the season, after all."

With a sigh, Dimitri cranked up the volume on the Christmas music. Stone mumbled something about the tree and left the room.

Later, after they'd gorged themselves on cookies and the tree was trimmed to the nines, Nik pulled Jess aside.

"What's next?" she asked, sounding more excited than she had when she'd arrived.

"Mitya's opening a bottle of wine and pulling out Cards Against Humanity."

"Oh, shit." She rubbed her hands together. "It's about to go down."

"We could play, if you want. Or..." His gaze shifted to the sliding glass doors that led outside. "It's cooled down a lot, but we do have a hot tub." He tried to keep his tone light and not suggestive. Whatever they did, it would be her choice.

Jess chewed her bottom lip for a moment, then nodded once. "Sure. I'll go put on my swimsuit."

Whoa. He'd half-expected her to tease him or turn him down. But no, she was grabbing her tote bag and disappearing into the hall bathroom.

Maybe it was wishful thinking, but he hoped it meant she was coming around to the idea of the two of them as a couple.

In his room, Nik changed into swim shorts and threw on a hoodie, leaving it unzipped. For the first and only time in his life, he wished he owned trunks that had a moose on them. Or more than one moose. He wasn't picky. As long as it made Jess smile.

Outside, he grabbed some towels from the shed and tossed them on the bench beside the hot tub, then cranked up the Jacuzzi jets. The water started bubbling, the oddly cozy smell of pool chemicals reaching his nostrils. He stripped off the hoodie and added it to the pile of towels. After the blast of cool night air, sliding into the water was pure bliss. He waited, just long enough to fret over whether Jess was punking him or not. When she appeared, he nearly choked. Her white bathing suit glowed in the soft yellow lights tucked in the foliage around the tub, and she was all strong, lean curves and shy smiles. With her hair braided around her head, she looked like a nymph stepping from the wilderness, or a goddess. She shivered and quickly slipped into the hot tub, sitting across from him.

She closed her eyes and leaned back, stretching her toned arms over the tiled edge. "This is nice."

"Yeah..." He couldn't help how dopey he sounded. Sitting in a hot tub with a beautiful woman whose company he enjoyed the hell out of was way more than *nice*.

They sat in silence, watching each other from across the water as the Jacuzzi jets hummed and the water bubbled.

Honesty had worked pretty well for him so far, so Nik spoke what was on the tip of his tongue.

"Jess?" His voice came out rough with desire. "I really want to kiss you again."

She sent him a small smile, her dimple winking at him. "I know."

She did? "How?"

"Because I want to kiss you, too."

Neither of them moved.

"I think we should wait until the next date," he said.

"Why?"

He swallowed, worried this would scare her off. It was a big move, and very soon, but he wanted to spend time with her far away from everything else, and he wanted to do it in the most picturesque and wintry locale he could manage within the confines of Southern California.

"I booked us a cabin at Big Bear," he said. Big Bear Lake, in the San Bernadino Mountains, was a year-round vacation spot, complete with hiking trails and ski resorts. The perfect place to experience the winter holidays, with the convenience of being just a few hours' drive from LA.

Jess's eyes went wide. "This late in the season? How did you manage? What did it cost?"

"Don't worry about that." He waved away those details. He'd spent half the morning on the phone to make it happen, and had agreed to stop by the birthday party of his agent's sister's seventh grader, a huge *Seize the Night* fan, but it had been worth it. Still, he wasn't sure what Jess's reaction meant. "Will you go with me?"

Her gaze focused on something in the distance over his shoulder as she thought about it.

"This is a big step," she said.

"Technically, our first kiss was almost a year ago. One could argue we're behind."

She gave him a bemused expression, and he held up his hands.

"Look," he said. "It's just one night, and the cabin has two bedrooms. I don't expect anything if you come with me. But they have snow there, real snow, and this whole endeavor just wouldn't be complete without a trip to a ski resort town decked out for the holidays."

She tilted her head and looked at him like she was seeing him for the first time. "You really do have a spirit of adventure, don't you?"

"There are many different kinds of adventures, Jeshka." Did she get what he meant? That he wanted her to be his next—and hopefully longest lasting—big adventure? He'd traveled the world, and he'd never felt as content as he did sitting in a hot tub with her, relaxing after a day with his friends and family. What else was there besides this? What else mattered?

Did he love his job? Of course he did. Getting paid good money to do something he excelled at was a blessing every day. But, if he were being honest, it was starting to get old. He was…tired.

Being with Jess revived him, rejuvenated him. With her by his side, he felt like he could tackle whatever the world threw at him.

What would he do if, at the end of all this, she told him to leave? Probably go on tour again, because there'd be no reason for him to stay here.

Except this time, he'd be leaving his heart here with her. Or maybe he'd already done that a year ago and hadn't even realized it.

He held back, hoping she understood him, not wanting to lay all his chips on the table just yet.

"You know what?" she said. "Fuck it."

She launched herself across the water at him, landing in his lap with her knees hugging his hips and her arms locking around his shoulders. Her mouth crushed down on his, the most delicious, wonderful, invigorating kind of ambush.

And the best kind of adventure.

———

THE JUXTAPOSITION of cool night air above and hot, bubbling water below heightened the sensory overload of Nik's lips and tongue moving over hers. Jess lost herself in his kiss, moaning when he nipped at her bottom lip and sucked lightly.

Under the water, his strong hands clamped on her ass, barely covered by the thin spandex of her swimsuit. He ran those clever fingers up her ribs to palm her breasts and his warm hands stroked her through the fabric, but it wasn't enough. She needed more contact. Breaking the kiss, she yanked at the ties holding the top of her suit up, then paused.

"What about the others?" she murmured. "What if they—?"

"They won't. Trust me."

Together, they pulled the fabric down to her waist. With nothing between them, Nik framed her breasts with his hands, rubbing his thumbs gently over her small brown nipples, which pebbled into hard peaks from his touch and the cool air. A tiny whimper squeezed from her throat as her body clenched with need.

His eyes were heavy-lidded and the tip of his tongue swiped back and forth across his lower lip. Anticipation hummed through her like a live wire. She wanted his mouth on her *now*.

"You're perfect," he whispered, awe in his voice.

All she could do to reply was thrust her chest toward his face in invitation.

With a low moan, Nik closed his mouth over one nipple and circled it with the tip of his tongue. She gasped and sank her fingers into his hair, holding him close as sensation streaked through her.

By the time Nik switched to her other breast, Jess was writhing on his lap, bucking her hips against him. Being with him like this, in the hot tub with his hands and mouth all over her, urged on by the feel of her core pressed up against his cock with only two thin layers of fabric separating them, was boiling her from the inside.

And she loved every second of it.

Her eyelids drifted closed and she let her head fall back, absorbing the pleasure he gave her. Waves of desire coursed through her in time with the rhythm of his tongue. Her body felt weightless, like she could float away at any moment.

But she wouldn't. He'd keep her anchored. In his arms, she was safe.

Nik raised his head. "Jess." Her name was like a whisper on the wind.

She opened her eyes and gazed down at him. "Hmm?" It was more a whine than a word, and he grinned.

"Can I touch you?"

A soft sigh escaped her parted lips, and once again, she brought her mouth to his. "I thought you'd never ask."

She kissed him, long and slow and soft, as he trailed his hand over her hip and down the crease of her thigh until he could position his thumb between her parted legs. In soft, slow motions, he stroked her through the fabric of her swimsuit.

Fireworks exploded beneath her skin at his touch.

He kept the rhythm steady and languid, even when she tried to urge him on with kisses and moans.

"Easy, Jeshka," he murmured against her lips. The nickname made her shiver. "No need to rush. We have all the time in the world." Then he took her mouth in a slow, drugging kiss.

With his other hand, he touched her breast and gently rubbed her nipple using the same unhurried timing. But his easy pace lit a fire in her. Her movements became more erratic. Her whimpers rose in volume and tempo. She didn't care who heard—not the neighbors, not their friends, not even his brother. The only things that mattered in this very moment were Nik's hands and Nik's mouth and that *he did not under any circumstances stop what he was doing.*

Finally, god, *finally*—he kicked up the pace, while still maintaining the same gentle pressure.

That was all she needed. With her lips pressed to his, she broke apart in his arms. As shock waves of pleasure soared through her body, he took her mouth in a searing kiss that swallowed her cries and fused the two of them even closer together than they'd been. Her hips rocked against his hand and her body shook with echoing surges of bliss.

When at last it was done, she rested her head on his broad shoulder.

For a long while, they stayed like that. Nik rubbed her back, his hands warming her cooling skin.

What. The Hell. Had just happened?

She'd been utterly consumed, just by his touch. And thanks to the heated water—and a brilliant orgasm—she couldn't even tell where she ended and he began. The edges of her body, of her being, felt fuzzy, like she was merging with him.

Her thoughts were thick as molasses, but that one made her attempt to sit up. When she stirred, she brushed against his hard-on.

"What about you?" she murmured, dropping her hand between them to stroke his cock through the swim trunks. He was heavy and hard, filling her hand in the most intriguing way.

"I'll survive." He kissed her sweetly. "Tonight was all about you."

She raised her head and looked him in the eye for a long moment. They'd crossed some bases tonight, but ever the gentleman, Nik was leaving it up to her to decide exactly how far they went. She licked her lips nervously, then asked a half question. "At the cabin?"

His cock jumped against her thigh like it understood what she meant. But Nik just nodded. "At the cabin."

Her eyelids drooped, but there was one more thing she needed to know. "Why did you ask me about this next one in advance? I already agreed to three dates."

He slid down a little to rest the back of his head against the lip of the tub. "I didn't want you to feel like I was tricking you into something you might not be comfortable with. I wanted to give you the opportunity to say yes or no."

The man's sweetness knew no bounds. What the hell was she supposed to say to that?

In a quiet voice, she said, "Thank you."

"You're welcome, milochka."

Another cute nickname. She wondered what it meant.

He swallowed hard, like he was unsure of himself. "So…you'll go with me?"

How could she say no?

"I will."

Chapter Six

December 22nd

The ride up to Big Bear was the most fun Jess had ever had being stuck in traffic. Nik sang her songs from the tours he'd done, and while he claimed he'd never be good enough for a leading role, she thought he sounded amazing. She wished she could see him perform on stage. He was so talented, it probably wouldn't be long before he had his next job lined up.

The thought made her sad, so she shoved it aside. Today was all about having fun, not thinking about his eventual departure.

Every so often, she'd look over at him driving, at ease behind the wheel of his brother's expensive SUV, and just admired his face.

It was a good face. He had good eyes, eyes that showered her with his undivided attention when she spoke—well, except for while he was driving, but he still darted looks at her and sent quick little grins her way.

He had a good mouth, too. A *very* good mouth. She ran her tongue over her lower lip, recalling his kisses. Maybe tonight she'd find out what else that mouth could do.

And then there were his hands, currently gripping the steering wheel as he navigated the freeway that would take them to Big Bear. Okay, so his hands weren't part of his face, but they were good hands—nay, *exceptionally* good hands. Her eyelids fluttered with remembered pleasure. Everything about their hot tub makeout session had been so perfect she almost wished someone had filmed it so she could relive it over and over and…

If he stayed, she wouldn't need a video of him to rub one out to. She'd have the real thing whenever she wanted it. If he stayed.

I'll stay, if you want me to.

Tonight was their last date. And then she'd have to decide if he'd pulled off a Christmas miracle after all and convinced her, a die-hard Scrooge, that dreams did come true, Christmas magic was real, and there were good men in this world who could be trusted to stick around.

When the next song ended, she gathered her courage and asked a question that had been on her mind since he'd popped into her life. "When was your last serious relationship?"

He used the steering wheel controls to lower the music volume, keeping his eyes on the road. "I had girlfriends when I lived in New York, but since then I haven't stayed in one place long enough for anything lasting, you know?"

The next question lodged in her throat, but she spoke it out loud anyway. "But you want that with me. Something 'lasting.'" Not a question, then. A clarification.

He cut his gaze to her and nodded once.

She let out a long breath as more questions bubbled up inside her. *Why the sudden shift?* she wanted to ask. *Why didn't you want it before? What's different now?* And most importantly, *Why me?* But those she held back. No matter what he said, there was still a good chance she wouldn't believe him.

"What about you?" he asked.

"You really want to know?"

"No." The corner of his mouth quirked. "But I figure you brought it up because you want to talk about it."

Shit, did she? Maybe he was right, because before she knew it, the words were coming out.

"I had a boyfriend in Chicago." She fiddled with her phone to give her hands something to do. "He was from the ballroom circuit. Not my partner, but someone I'd known for a while. We dated for a couple years."

She pressed her lips together, because the next part would give away too much. He gave her a *go on* kind of look, and with a sigh, she did.

"He moved away, to New York. To 'make it.'"

Nik sighed. "If you can make it there, you can make it anywhere. Or so I've heard."

"I wouldn't know."

"Is that why you moved to LA?"

"Partly. After he left, there was really nothing for me in Chicago, and I was miserable living at home."

"Why not New York?"

"By the time I'd saved up enough to move, he wasn't there anymore. He'd landed a contract with a cruise ship company, and now he lives in Florida."

"I see."

And the thing was, he probably did. But not the whole picture. She let out a long breath, then launched into her sad, sorry history. "He wasn't the only guy who left."

"No?" He glanced over at her, eyebrow raised.

Something about talking to him while he drove was easier. Maybe because he couldn't stare her down with those soulful brown eyes that urged her to reveal all her secrets. Now, without their powerful gaze turned on her, it was almost like she was just talking to herself.

"My dad," she said, then interrupted herself. "Look, I know where my baggage comes from. It's not like I'm unaware."

Nik didn't comment on that. "What about your dad?"

"Nothing major," she said with a shrug. "We didn't have a ton of money, and being a competitive dancer isn't cheap, as I'm sure you know. He and my mom used to fight all the time, and some-times he'd leave for a while. He always came back, but then they'd go through the cycle all over again. And it...it happened a lot around the holidays. The extra stress of that time of year made their relationship worse, so he'd leave, and then my mom would get depressed and not decorate. That's the real reason why we didn't always have a Christmas tree. It was hard to focus on holiday cheer when we were all wondering if this was the time he never came back."

Nik was quiet for a moment. "Where is he now?"

"At home, with my mom." At his confused look, she let out a resigned chuckle. "I know. It's so weird. They're like best friends now. I guess being parents and being a couple was too much for them at the same time. Now that they can just focus on each other, they're fine."

"Jess...that's not your fault."

"Oh, I know." She forced her tone to be light, because she *did* know, intellectually. "But I carry the baggage with me all the same. I tried to leave it behind in Chicago, but would you look at that, it followed me all the way to Los Angeles."

They drove in silence for a few minutes, long enough for Jess to beat herself up over saying anything in the first place. She opened her mouth to break the silence—a subject change, a bad joke, anything—when Nik reached over and took her hand. He laced their fingers together, rested their joined hands on his thigh, and then turned up the radio volume and began to sing along with a well-known Broadway showtune about friendship.

And just like that, she felt okay again.

What's more, she felt...freer. Less burdened by memories. Over the last week, it had gotten easier to open up to Nik. He was a good listener, and aside from some light teasing about being a Scrooge, he didn't judge her. Speaking her pain out loud and having him understand eased some of the pressure she carried in her heart.

And maybe made a little space for him in there, too.

Once they arrived at Big Bear, Jess could see why he'd brought her. There was Christmas shit *everywhere*. It was like a freaking Christmas town. And while she giggled over the absurdity of it all, a small part of her was charmed.

Okay, a big part.

Fine, *all* of her found it charming. But that was probably just because she was with Nik. He loved Christmas so much, it was impossible not to get caught up in his enthusiasm.

All the same, she looked forward to getting to their cabin, where it would be just the two of them, alone.

Tonight was the night. She was going to have sex with Nik Kovalenko.

Just the thought of it sent a thrill of desire coursing through her.

But first, Nik had a whole list of Christmassy shit for them to do. Photos with Santa, ice skating, tubing, even a damned alpine slide. An early dinner at a beautiful restaurant that overlooked Big Bear Lake, followed by something called Santa's Hayride to the North Pole, which was as charming as it was weird.

She would have rolled her eyes and demanded he cut to the chase, the chase being his dick, but she was having the time of her life. Not only that, Nik took every opportunity to touch her. He held her hand in the car while stuck in stop-and-go traffic on the freeway. He pressed a light touch to her lower back to shift her away from bumping into a child at Santa's village. Activities like the alpine slide and tubing required closeness, and he cuddled against her as much as he was able. While ice skating, he only released her to show off some moves, and then she showed off some of her own.

The touches were so light, so innocent.

So why the fuck were they igniting a raging fire of lust inside her?

Their makeout session in the hot tub kept flashing through her mind. Sex with Nik was going to be *excellent*.

But deep down, she knew this wasn't just about playing anymore. Her damned heart was involved.

You hush, she told her heart. *This is not heart time. This is coochie time.*

But no matter what she told herself, Nik's Christmas magic seeped into her and made her consider what the future might hold for them.

When they pulled up to the cabin, it was like something out of a dream. All warm, weathered wood, peaked roof, and a covered front porch. Colorful lights sparkled in the bushes and a wreath covered half the front door. A sprinkling of snow added to the already-picturesque image. The sight calmed her, somewhat.

And then, as if he could tell she was nervous, Nik turned to her the moment the door closed behind them. Settling his hands on her shoulders, he looked deep into her eyes and said, "I'll open some wine."

She nodded, and then she finally took a good look around. The cabin was fully decorated, with branches of pine and holly, twinkling white lights, and festive red-and-gold ribbons. A small Christmas tree sat in one corner, and two stockings even hung from the fireplace mantle. The whole place smelled like pine—real pine—and cinnamon.

The halls, as they say, were *decked.*

Jess followed Nik into the open kitchen space where he drew a bottle of Prosecco from the half-fridge under the counter. An explosion of white and red roses sat in a vase on top, scenting the air. "Do the cabins come pre-decorated this time of year?"

He chuckled. "No, just the outside, although that would be smart."

"So, who did all this?" she asked, gesturing at the tree and roses.

There was a muffled whoosh and a pop as Nik opened the Prosecco, catching the cork in a dishtowel. "I did."

She could have sworn the floor just rocked beneath her feet—

not an impossibility in California, but in this instance the sensation was caused by his words. "Come again?"

"I came up here yesterday to set up." He poured the sparkling, fizzing liquid into two champagne flutes. When he handed her one, she took it automatically, too stunned by his sweet admission to do much else. Then he met her gaze, tapped his glass to hers, and murmured, "Cheers."

The word trembled through her, deep and full of promise. She hurried to take a sip. Promises were easy to make. Keeping them was another story.

But so far, even she had to admit Nik was as good as his word. Somehow, between sipping hot chocolate at the mall while snow bubbles floated around them, baking inappropriate cookies with his family and friends, and entering a Christmas cabin decked out like something in a movie, she had found the sense of comfort that came with such trappings. He'd made her believe.

Not only that, he made her feel special, made her feel like she belonged. For a girl who'd grown up thinking she didn't fit in, who liked strange things none of her peers liked, who traveled often for competitions and didn't hold onto friends, it was a giddy feeling that went straight to her head, like the Prosecco.

Nik pressed something on his phone, and music began to play softly in the background. The piano notes swirled around them, soon joined by a subtle string accompaniment.

"Is this 'Have Yourself a Merry Little Christmas?'" Jess asked. This version was romantic, if a tad obvious.

"Mm-hmm." He took their glasses and set them on the counter. And then, as if it were the most natural thing in the world, he slipped his right arm around her, took her right hand with his left, and swept them into a Viennese waltz.

Oh. He'd remembered.

The sweetness of the moment soared through her, merging with the special place this dance style had always held in her heart.

As they traced through the turns, change steps, and reverse

turns, following the *one-two-three* pattern like it was something they'd been born to do together, the music cast a spell around them. It was the most sensual rendition of the song she'd ever heard, moody and ethereal. The soaring vocals wrapped around them as they moved in unison, turning and reversing in a circuit around the spacious kitchen, their stocking feet shuffling lightly on the tile floor. Nik led them into a six-step fleckerl spin, stopped with a smooth contra check, then sent them spinning the other way.

Every time he twirled her out and brought her back in, it was a relief to be in closed hold with him again. He maintained perfect control, perfect speed, and kept his eyes on hers, except to check the space around them.

The beauty of the moment, of the dance, brought tears to her eyes. The waltz had a reputation for being boring or old-fashioned, but to her, there was freedom in the swirling, never-ending movement, a comforting solidity in the hold, and an exuberance in the rise and fall as they rotated around the space.

Dancing with this man was a dream come true. Everything he was came through in the dance—steady, solid, *true*. Leading, but gently. With an innate connection to her own rhythm and movement, matching her steps and her momentum. The perfect balance. The perfect partner.

She never wanted this to end.

But the song did end, with a long, soulful note, and Nik brought them to rest where they'd started, right next to their glasses. Without taking his gaze from hers, he handed her the drink.

Her heart was in her throat and in her eyes. The magic of the day was getting to her. Or maybe it was the Prosecco. She took another sip, then set the glass aside again. No, it wasn't the Prosecco. It was Nik. He'd given her three dates, doing everything in his power to help her enjoy the holiday season and showing her his true self in the process.

It would take a stronger woman than she to resist all that.

She slipped her fingers into the waistband of his jeans and tugged him closer.

"No mistletoe?" she teased.

"If I have to trick you into kissing me, I'm doing something wrong." He drained his glass, put it on the counter, and cupped her face with both hands. His eyes smoldered, the amber color hot and dreamy, like smooth caramel.

"You tasted like champagne the first time we kissed," he said in a low voice.

"And potato chips." Her reminder was nothing more than a murmur, but his lips curved.

"Sour cream and onion," he said. And then his mouth came down on hers, and it was everything she'd waited for all day, all *year*. God, yes, she'd been waiting all year to be with this man. How had she refrained from jumping on him the second she'd seen him in that silly shirt with the ornaments hooked to it? *Why* had she? Instead of dragging him into a hallway to ask why he was commenting on her pictures, she should have found a dark room and had her way with him. His mouth, his lips, his touch... were *everything*. The way he savored and sipped at her—but with an edge, as if his slow movements masked a raging sense of hunger—stoked her own desire to a fever pitch.

Heat rushed through her as she slipped her hands under his shirt and traced her fingers over his abs, like she'd done in the hot tub. He broke the kiss to rip the shirt over his head and toss it aside.

"Your body is amazing," she said, the words ending on a groan as her hands roamed his exposed skin, outlining the hard lines, curves, bumps, and angles of his body.

He laughed under his breath and trailed his fingers down her ribcage. "That's my line, milochka."

The term of endearment gave her shivers. "Now you've done it. I'm going to need you to whisper sweet nothings in my ear."

He bent closer, and as his hands stroked her body, he unleashed a sensuous stream of Russian. The unfamiliar syllables fell from his mouth in a deep, dark rumble, like approaching thunder. His lips tickled her ear and his breath caressed her neck, heating her from the inside out. The subtle scent of his cologne and the sharp freshness of the Prosecco drugged her senses. She stood in the middle of a storm, powerless against the crush of sensations and emotions tangling within her, toppling all her last defenses.

Without her walls, without her guards, it was just the two of them. And finally, *finally*, she could just sink into the moment with him and *be*.

When she threw her arms over his shoulders and leaned into him, he lifted her up. Their mouths fused, her legs locked around his hips, and she whispered one word against his lips: "Bed."

————

IN THE CABIN'S master bedroom, Nik laid her on the bed with care, as if she were made of the finest spun glass. To him, she was just as precious.

At first, he was content to just lie beside her, kissing languidly. But spinning her around the kitchen for their waltz had been all sorts of foreplay, and she'd already gotten him out of his shirt. He wanted to touch her, too.

His lips stayed on hers as he skimmed his fingers under the bright orange sweater she wore, enjoying the feel of her warm, smooth skin. Slowly, he edged the fabric up, revealing a lacy black bralette.

Groaning, he traced his fingertips over the lace, warmed by her body. Jess pulled off the sweater and her hands went to the button on her jeans, but he stopped her.

"Ne speshi," he murmured, urging her to slow down. Everything else with them was a rush, but he wanted this to last. He wanted to savor every sensation, every sound, every touch. He wanted to imprint something lasting in her memory, to show her that she could trust herself with him, even in this.

In his eyes, she was worthy of worship, of appreciation, and he would use every tool at his disposal to show her how he felt, even pleasure.

He bent and tongued her nipple through the lace. Holding her in his arms while she gasped and twisted in pleasure was the best thing he could have ever imagined. Her lithe body responded to his every touch, and like a dance, her moves called forth answering waves of arousal in him.

Covering her body in kisses and caresses, he managed to remove both their pants. Clad only in boxers, he sat up and unzipped a small pouch sitting on the side table, revealing condoms, lube, a silk blindfold, and a small, bullet-shaped magenta vibrator. When Jess shot him a surprised look, he jerked one shoulder, suddenly feeling awkward. "I didn't know what you preferred, so I wanted to have some options."

Her gaze softened. "Are you this thoughtful about everything?"

"I try." His tone was serious. "I don't jump into things lightly, Jeshka."

From the look in her eyes, she got that he was talking about *them*. About the intention he'd declared at the mall.

"I've had all year to think about it," he said, setting the bag aside to smooth his hands over her body.

"All…all year?" Her voice trembled as he pinched the sides of her panties and pulled them down her hips inch by agonizing inch, savoring the view as she was revealed to him.

"Mm-hmm." He made a low sound of appreciation in the back of his throat. When the last scrap of fabric was gone, he trailed his fingers lightly over her bare mound. "So pretty."

She huffed out an awkward laugh. "It's more for convenience, but whatever you say, you beautiful man."

He shot her a grin, then slid out of his own underwear so they were both completely naked. Settling between her thighs, he traced a finger down her crease, appreciating the soft moan she made in response.

"It took me a while to recognize what I wanted. It wasn't until I saw Mitya and Tash that I knew."

She threw a hand over her eyes. "Are you really talking about your brother at a time like this?"

He kept going, sliding his index finger inside her just enough to tease. She was so smooth, so beautiful, and already wet. "I saw them and thought, maybe settling down can be an adventure, too. And it made me think of you."

A hitch in her breath was his only answer. He looked up.

"Jeshka."

"Huh?"

"Uncover your eyes."

With a groan, she pulled her arm from across her face and gazed down at him. Her dark eyes were drowsy, her brown skin warm with pleasure.

"I want you, Jeshka. Not just for now."

Did she understand what he meant? Could she see the love shining in his face? Her eyebrows shifted the barest fraction, and something like fear flitted through her eyes. Yes, love was scary. *Forever* was scary. But he was willing to face it, with her. For her.

He wouldn't push, though. Sliding her knee up, he kissed down the inside of her thigh. "Ah, milochka. You take my breath away."

Her voice was muffled, like she'd turned her face into the pillow. "Don't say things like that."

"Like what?"

"Sweet things."

"Why not?"

"I don't...I don't know. I'm not used to hearing them."

At that, he crawled up her body so he could kiss her lips and look her in the eye. "I'm not those other guys, Jeshka. I'm not gonna hit it and quit it. Okay?"

When she nodded, he moved back down her body and resumed what he'd been doing.

"You don't have to say anything now," he continued. "I'm just letting you know, because my mouth is about to be very busy."

Then he parted her sex with his thumbs and got to it.

———

JESS THREW her head back on the pillow. This man was impossible. Saying every kind of thing a person could want to hear, and then, without wasting another second, lowering his head and eating her pussy for all he was worth.

That mouth. If she'd known he was that skilled with his lips, with his tongue, she never would have given him such pushback.

Stupid Past Jessica. She should have pulled him into Rhianne's office, stripped out of her clothes, and told him to do what he did best. Because as amazing as he was as a dancer, *this* was his true calling.

But the things he'd been saying... Such simple words, yet they'd affected her like the filthiest of dirty talk. Except instead of only arousing of her body, they also roused her heart.

And now that treacherous thing was fully, irrevocably involved.

He claimed to have been thinking about them becoming an *us* all year, since their first kiss. She'd thought it was a throwaway kiss for him. A kiss of convenience. It had been New Year's Eve, almost midnight, and she was the handiest pair of lips nearby. Afterward, when she'd found herself thinking about him before falling asleep, she'd convinced herself that it meant nothing to her, either. It was fun. A lark. Nothing more.

What if it wasn't?

I want you, Jeshka. Not just for now.

I'll stay, if you want me to.

The words had burrowed into her heart and made themselves at home. She'd never be the same after this. Because what else did he mean, if not "just for now"? For...

For...what?

Always? Ever?

He couldn't mean *that*. Who said such things on a third date? She wanted to shut her eyes—against him, against the thought— but even as his tongue swirled over her clit, he held her gaze. The sincerity in his eyes sank into her with a bone-deep surety.

This man was the real deal.

Then he closed his lips over her clit and sucked, making her cry out as his mouth sent buzzing thrills of sensation through her.

After that, thinking was hard. So she stopped.

Nik's sweet, lingering touches turned hotter, more demanding. His kisses took on an edgy, erotic note that left her breathless. And his mouth must have covered every inch of her skin. When he finally slipped on a condom and rubbed some lube over it, she was nearly mindless with need. Her breath expelled from her lungs in harsh exhalations, anticipation steaming through her veins like a runaway freight train.

"Jeshka."

Oh god, the way he said her name like that. It would be her undoing.

"Come on," he said, reclining on the bed beside her. "Get on me."

Those had to be the hottest words she'd ever heard. Renewed by the prospect of finally feeling him inside her, she rose up and straddled his hips. He rubbed his cock against her slit, making her gasp. No more wasting time. No more games. This was happening *now*.

She positioned herself on his length and sank down, engulfing him with her body, impaling herself with his. Her slick, tight sheath stretched around him, and he filled her so completely, so deliciously. Pleasure shot through her, and when she finally came to a stop with her clit resting against his root, a shiver raced up her spine. His laugh was low, and she realized she'd closed her eyes again. Opening them, she couldn't help but stroke his handsome face. His facial hair was soft, but still prickled her palm. One of these days, she'd ask how he conditioned it. For now, she had more important things to do.

Rocking back and forth, she built up friction between them until they were both groaning. Nik's strong hands clamped on her ass to help her move. As easy as dancing, they set a rhythm between them, making their own music together. He slipped his thumb between her legs, rubbing her as they moved. Her hands went wild, touching every bit of his body she could reach. He did the same with his free hand, stroking over her breasts, hips, thighs, even up her neck to cup her cheek. He pulled her down to kiss him, and she kissed him back with a desperation she'd never felt before as the mix of emotions he stirred up in her became too much to bear. He banded his arms around her, pulling her down to his body. His hips pumped like pistons, driving upward into her.

Tension built inside her, coiling in her muscles. Her body strained, her heart pleaded, and then, finally, the orgasm burst through her. Like sunlight piercing a cloud, like sparkles behind closed eyelids, like a swiftly beating heart, it chased away the shadows and for one brief, stunning moment, she achieved perfect clarity.

She never wanted this to stop. She never wanted to let him go.

What if he meant it? What if he was really planning to stay, if she asked?

Did she even have the guts to ask such a thing?

She wanted to, oh god, she really fucking wanted to. This was too good. Everything about him was too good. And in her experience, things that seemed "too good" were, by extension, "too good to be true."

But if anyone were true, it was Nik.

She couldn't ask yet. Not yet, not now. It was too good, too *much*, and she was going out of her mind with want and need for him. More, yes, she did want more. She wanted everything. And the depth of the wanting scared the pants off her.

Focus on the here, the now. Focus on the moment. It wasn't just games and fun anymore. This was serious, but still, she could focus on how good it felt, how *right* it felt, and forget about the rest, forget about the future, for now. Was this part of the magic of Christmas? Enjoying the last days of the year, living in the moment, before stepping over the threshold into a new year with new resolutions, responsibilities, and consequences?

If so, then she'd embrace it. For now, right now, everything was perfect and beautiful. And she'd snatch it up with both hands.

The thoughts lasted a split second, chased by the flow of good endorphins. Beneath her, Nik slammed her hips down on himself one last time, then lifted her off him. Quick as a wink, he tore off the condom, jerked his cock in his hand a few times, and came with a groan all over his own belly.

The tension in his body, his grimace of ecstasy, and the evidence of his pleasure—it was the sexiest fucking thing she'd ever seen.

His chest heaved, making his defined abdominal muscles contract with every breath. His head fell back on the pillow.

She slid down next to him and rubbed his chest, needing to prolong the contact, enjoying the simple pleasure of watching him breathe. When had she become so damned sentimental? It was probably Christmas's fault. The room was quiet, aside from the sounds of their breathing. From the floor, something buzzed.

"Was that the vibrator?" she asked sleepily.

Under her ear, his laugh rumbled through his chest. "My phone. Ignore it."

"No, you should check," she said, pushing herself up on her elbows. "Go ahead. It might be important."

With a sigh that said he was only humoring her, he reached over the edge of the bed to grab his phone out of his pants pocket. She admired his sculpted ass and the long stretch of tightly muscled body as he moved. Leaning back, he held the phone over his face and narrowed his eyes at the screen.

He was silent for so long, she started to get nervous. "Everything okay?" she asked lightly.

"Yeah, just my agent." He set the phone on the nightstand and turned back to embrace her, but paused, glancing down at the streaks drying on his belly. "I need to clean off."

"We both do." The inside of her thighs felt sticky, but more than that, the thought of showering with him appealed immensely.

But his reaction to the phone bothered her, and she couldn't let it go. "So…what did your agent say?"

"Just reminding me I have to give him an answer."

Her breath caught. She struggled to keep her tone as casual as the hand he rubbed along her back. It moved in a lazy circuit from her shoulders down the curve of her butt, and back up again. "An answer about what?"

"I got offered a role," he said quietly, almost nonchalantly. Like it didn't matter, like he got offered roles every day.

Hell, maybe he did.

"Oh yeah?" When he didn't elaborate, she pressed. "What role?"

This had suddenly become the most important conversation she'd ever had.

"Pete Oliynyk in *Raise Your Voice*. They want me to be dance captain in the national tour."

Holy shit.

Raise Your Voice was currently the hottest show on Broadway, a timely true story about a diverse group of teens fighting for immigration reform. Tickets were expensive, and you had to buy them over a year in advance. She hadn't even known it was going on tour.

But of course it was. And of course they'd tap Nik, a rising star, to play one of the bigger side characters, with the added honor of being dance captain. As an immigrant himself, the role likely meant something personal to him. There was no way he could turn it down.

How long had he known about this?

She swallowed hard. He was leaving. He *had* to. This was the kind of opportunity he'd be stupid to pass up, no matter what he said about *them* or *us*.

There was no them. There couldn't be. Because if it wasn't this tour, it would be another one. He was too talented to interrupt his career for *her*.

Somewhere along the way, she'd forgotten that this was just supposed to be for fun.

His hand on her back slowed, and turned his head toward her. His gaze held a question.

I'll stay, if you want me to.

"New Year's Eve," she whispered, feeling sick inside. She'd give him his answer then.

That would at least buy her some time to convince her heart that letting him go was best for both of them.

Chapter Seven

December 23rd

T he next morning, the light seeping around the edges of the curtains had a distinct quality, soft and sort of dreamy, like…

Nik bolted out of the bed. It had been years since he'd lived full time in New York City, but this sort of light could only mean one thing.

He threw open the curtains, raised the blinds, and sure enough…

"Snow!"

Jess groaned and rolled over, snagging his pillow and pulling it over her satin-covered head. Last night, she'd explained the importance of a satin headscarf and pillowcase—she'd brought her own —to hair care. He'd filed the information away, wondering if it would be presumptuous of him to buy her a spare pillowcase for his place. Except his place was currently his brother's place. Hmm, he'd have to fix that soon. For now, he turned back to the window.

Outside, a blanket of snow covered everything—the trees, the driveway, his car, the roads…

Shit, the roads.

"I hope you didn't have anything pressing to do today," he told the lump in the blankets. "I'm pretty sure the roads are going to be closed for a while."

One word drifted from the bed, delivered like a grumpy command: "Coffee."

Grinning, Nik knelt on the mattress and dropped a kiss around where he thought her head would be. Then he pulled on his boxers and ambled out of the room. To say he was feeling like a million bucks would have been an understatement. And maybe it was sappy of him, but as much as he'd loved being with her, sinking into her and being as close as two people could be, it was the simple act of holding her through the night while she slept that brought him the greatest pleasure.

Yeah, he was a sap. Who could blame him? It was nearly Christmas, and he was snowed in with the most intriguing, beautiful, and funny woman he'd ever met.

In the kitchen, he used the French press he'd brought with him to brew coffee. While he waited, he shot an email to his agent, telling him to turn down the *Raise Your Voice* role. He'd made his decision. Jess might need a little more time, but he wasn't giving up on her. Or himself—he'd committed to giving this "settling down" thing a try, and so, he was staying. Putting down roots. This was Los Angeles—local opportunities were sure to pop up. But, to respect Jess's wishes, he'd wait until New Year's Eve to discuss it further.

When the coffee was ready, he prepped it the way he knew she liked it and carried the mug into the bedroom.

He was all set to climb back into the bed with her for a morning cuddle, but when she heard him, she sat up and reached for the mug. She took a big gulp, then sent him a sleepy smile. "Thanks."

"Anytime."

She sipped again, then straightened her headscarf, which had gone crooked while she slept. "Did you say the roads are closed?"

"I think so." He tapped his phone. "There was an inclement weather alert for this area last night."

Her eyes widened. "Are we snowed in?"

"Looks that way."

She shook her head and mumbled into her mug, "This is just like a movie."

He laughed, then started to lean in to kiss her, but she slid out of the bed and headed for the bathroom. "I'm gonna shower," she said. Before he could reply, the door shut behind her.

Well. Okay. So she wasn't a morning person. She'd told him that on the first date. And there was bound to be some awkwardness during the first morning after.

The night before had been...amazing. No other word to describe it. Everything he'd traveled the world searching for, he'd found in being with Jess. A sense of peace, freedom, contentment, and belonging, all rolled up into something that seemed to point toward love. What else could it be?

She'd been there every step of the way with him while they'd been having sex, that was for sure. Her kisses told the truth. But what if that was all they had? He'd set out to be as open as he could with her, to not hold back. Go big or go home, right? But after days of wearing his heart on his sleeve, his vulnerability gas tank was on empty.

Maybe he'd been fooling himself all along. He didn't think so, and he was a pretty good judge of character—he'd been the first one to tell Dimitri to get his head out of his ass where Natasha was concerned—but doubts had started to creep in after he'd told Jess what was up last night and her only reply had been, "New Year's Eve." After that, they'd gone into the bathroom to clean up, then finished the Prosecco and roasted marshmallows in the fire he built in the fireplace. He'd also pulled out a bag of sour cream and onion potato chips—a nod to their first kiss.

It was nice. Romantic. But Jess hadn't brought up any of the things he'd said. Not the tour, and not his "not just for now" line. Probably he could've phrased that better, and maybe he shouldn't have said it *during* sex, but it aligned with everything else he'd told her since seeing her at Rhianne's party, so it shouldn't have been a surprise. Yet he could feel her putting distance between them, and he had no idea how to stop it.

Damn, what if she still didn't believe him? What if he'd put it all on the line, bared his heart and soul, to no avail?

There was still the possibility that this gamble wouldn't pay off, that he wouldn't be able to convince her. Shit, that he *hadn't* been able to convince her. This was the last date.

At the start, he'd been sure it was worth a try. And he still felt that way. But he was a big enough person to admit his feelings were a little bruised.

The snow had bought him a little more time, and a little more holiday magic. He'd make the most of it, and then…well, it was all up to Jess.

His phone rang in the kitchen and he hurried to pick it up.

It was his mother, Oksana. Jess was still in the bathroom, so he accepted the call and held the phone to his ear. "Hey, mamochka. What's up?"

She talked to him in Russian about their upcoming Christmas plans, his cousin Alex's pregnant wife, and his dad's latest wood-working project. While she spoke, Nik got an idea. He outlined it for his mother in Russian.

"Listen, mamochka, I'm seeing this woman, and she's really special to me. If I can convince her to come, I want to bring her home with me for the holidays."

Oksana was, predictably, overjoyed that her second wayward son appeared to be settling down with "a nice girl." Of course Nik could bring her to Christmas with the family.

After he hung up, the bedroom door opened and Jess emerged fully dressed. When she saw him, her shoulders stiffened.

It was a slight move, but he caught it. Something was definitely up. So instead of asking if she wanted to spend the holidays with his family, he said, "You wanna play in the snow?"

She glanced down at his boxers, the only thing he had on, and raised an eyebrow. "Don't you think you'll be a little cold?"

"I'll get dressed."

"Cool. I'll make breakfast." She brushed past him to open the fridge.

Cool, indeed. Her demeanor had taken a turn toward frosty, at complete odds with the heat they'd generated the previous night. If only he had some idea of what was going on in that pretty head of hers, but if he asked, she'd just deflect with a question of her own.

With a sinking feeling in the pit of his stomach, he got dressed to go out in the snow.

———

PLAYING IN THE SNOW. At their age. But this was why Jess had agreed to the whole "holiday dates" endeavor in the first place—to have fun. To prove to herself and Naomi that she did know how to play. So, play in the snow they would.

Besides, it would keep her mind off everything Nik had revealed the night before.

The feelings stirred up by having sex with him were stronger than she'd ever felt, stronger than she was comfortable with, and she was already scared by how much she'd gotten used to spending time with him. They were having the kinds of deep conversations people didn't usually have after a few dates, at least not in her experience. If she were being honest, the depth of Nik's devotion scared her a little. What on earth had she done to deserve it? And she was no prude, but sleeping next to someone for the first time was a huge leap in intimacy. She liked it, secretly craved it, but she still didn't trust it, or herself.

And when he left? What then?

Because he was going to leave. She was sure of it now. The *Raise Your Voice* opportunity was too big, too good, to pass up.

Maybe he'd be back later, but she hadn't been kidding when

she said she wasn't going to wait around for him. For one thing, her heart wouldn't be able to withstand missing him so much. And for another, she'd just be waiting for him to leave again.

Been there, done that. She was so completely over waiting for the important men in her life to decide whether they wanted to stay or go.

So, this snow thing was good. It would distract her from everything else she couldn't figure out.

First step: snowman.

After agreeing on an ideal spot, they began packing the snow to build the body. They worked well together, which shouldn't have been a surprise, considering how well they danced together. He took her suggestions and gave feedback, maintaining light conversation and good humor. They'd both grown up in places that got a lot of snow, so it brought up a lot of nostalgia.

"Mitya and our older cousins always beat me in snowball fights," Nik said, placing the snowman's head on top of the body.

"Really?" That gave her an idea.

"Yeah, they were a lot older than I was, and I was little. Probably we played in the snow back in Ukraine, but I don't remember it, and we don't have many pictures from that time."

There was something in his voice that made her pause. "Do you miss it?" she asked.

He shrugged. "Nothing to miss. I was only a baby when we moved, and no else really talks about it. When they do, it's not fondly, not like 'the good old days.' They left everything behind for a reason, and no one seems inclined to reminisce over it."

"I can see that," she said, thinking about what it must have been like for him, growing up in a new place that was all he'd ever known, but that was so different for everyone else in his family. Maybe he didn't miss being there, but she would wager there was still a sense of missing something, even if it was just missing memories. "My mom and sister laugh about the times my dad was gone, and the fights that led to his leaving. I guess it's their way of making peace with the past, but I just want to forget about it."

"Everyone processes differently," he said in a quiet voice.

She nodded. The vibe had turned somber, so she changed the subject to lighten the mood.

"Our snowman needs a name," she said as she packed more snow onto the torso.

"Who says it's a man? What do we humans know about snow-people genders?"

She huffed out a laugh. "Fine, we'll give our snowperson a gender neutral name. Something cool."

"How about...Leslie."

"Cooler than that."

"Okay, you pick a name."

She thought for a moment. "What about Alex?"

"Nope. That's my cousin's name."

"Hmm. Charlie?"

"Is that a cool name?"

"I don't know. Devon?"

"Maybe." He sent her a sly grin. "How about Jessie?"

She kicked some snow at him. "That's my name!"

He snapped his fingers. "I've got it. Frances."

"No!" She kicked more snow, giggling her head off.

"Mackenzie?"

She stopped laughing and pursed her lips in thought. "You know what? I like it. Mackenzie Snow."

"Perfect."

"What are we going to use for the face?"

"I'll go find something."

The second he turned away, she scooped up a handful of snow, expertly packed it into a ball, and let it fly. It hit him square in the center of his back with a splat.

He froze, then turned around with a mixture of disbelief and humor on his face. His gaze tracked the snow at his feet, but then he looked back at her, still frozen.

Aww, that was sweet. He was hesitant to hit her with a snow-ball. His chivalry would be his downfall.

Ducking behind the snowman, she packed another snowball and threw. He dodged this one, then charged at her. With a squeal, she took off across the expanse of snow, giggling and trying to scoop up another handful as she went.

A snowball hit the back of her head and she shrieked. "My hair!"

She turned to see his look of horror. Little did he know, her hair was safely braided and protected by a satin cap inside her knit hat. She used the distraction to throw the snowball hidden in her hand. Nik tried to move, but was too late. The snowball caught him in the neck.

He hissed, trying to keep the snow from trickling down his collar. "That was a dirty move," he called.

She just threw another one at him.

He charged her again, and this time she wasn't fast enough to get away. With a soft tackle, he took them both down into a pile of untouched snow.

She lost it, giggling uncontrollably. This was too much fun. The snow was cold against her back, but the sun was warm on her face, Nik's body was solid on top of hers, and she was overheated from layers and exertion. Nik rose over her. The adoration in his face scared her a little. What did you do when you'd never bothered to imagine the man of your dreams, yet he showed up anyway?

A twitch at the corner of his mouth was the only warning she got before a handful of snow landed on her face. As she sputtered amid bursts of laughter, his lips found hers, and then they were kissing and grinding against each other through all the layers of clothing. She couldn't feel him through the fabric, through the insulated gloves covering her fingers. And she wanted, needed, to feel him.

"Inside," she gasped against his lips. "Take me inside." *I need you inside me.*

She wasn't ready to make a decision about the future yet, but neither was she ready to let this—or him—go.

NIK SPRANG TO HIS FEET, hauling Jess into his arms and continuing to kiss her as he tromped through the snow toward the cabin's back door.

Poor Mackenzie the Snowperson would just have to live without a face.

Inside, they left a trail of clothing from the back door, starting with their snowy boots and ending with their underwear by the side of the bed.

Jess reached for the pouch he'd packed, but instead of pulling out a condom, she held up the vibrator and sent him a saucy little smile.

As much as he was worried about these swings in her mood— cool one moment, hot the next—he couldn't resist her. He would give her anything she wanted.

They sprawled naked on the bed, kissing with feverish intensity. Nik took the vibrator from her, but before he could turn it on, she pushed him back onto the pillows and shimmied down his body until her face was level with his jutting cock.

She sent him a wink, and just like that, closed those luscious lips of hers over his dick, enveloping him in warm, tight heat.

Nik let out a long, low groan as she slicked her mouth over him, getting him good and wet. She gave a questioning little moan in reply and squeezed the base of his dick with her fist.

God, she was so feisty. He loved that about her.

Her tongue laved over him, her eyes shot him amorous looks from under her lashes, and all he could do was cup the back of her neck and *feel*.

With her hands and mouth, she pumped him, simulating what he wanted to do to her. Tension coiled in his muscles, the need to spill in her mouth taunting him. He held it back. Despite how utterly fucking amazing her mouth—and oh god, her *tongue*—felt on and around his cock, he wanted more. When he could take it no longer, he hauled her up to kiss her.

"That's enough," he said, panting. "Now it's your turn."

He popped his index finger into his mouth to get it wet and slid his hand over the smooth mound of her sex. Stroking gently, he slipped his finger between her folds and into her. She clung to his shoulders, gasping his name in his ear. It was the most beautiful sound he'd ever heard.

But as much as he tried to lose himself in her body, in the heat they generated together, he couldn't stop thinking about wanting more. Wanting her to give up this "kiss at New Year's Eve" farce, wanting to feel comfortable asking her to come visit his family with him, simply because he didn't want to be apart from her. But yeah, also because he wanted her to meet his family, and for them to meet her and love her as much as he already did.

He loved her, and holding it back was like death by a thousand paper cuts.

But if he told her now, he'd scare her off. She was already guarded. Behind the veneer of snark, she kept her heart locked away.

So he told her with his mouth, his hands, his body. He told her with slow, drugging kisses and smooth, sure strokes. When he rolled on a condom and sank into her wet heat, he told her with his moves, with the rhythm, with the way he held her close.

Something in the sheets bumped his arm and he glanced over to see what it was. Shit, they'd forgotten about the vibrator. Just the thought of using it on her made his pulse leap.

Withdrawing from her body, Nik shifted so he was sitting on the edge of the bed, then positioned her on his lap, facing away from him.

She mumbled something that sounded like "yes, please," then gripped his thighs for leverage. Raising her hips, seated herself on his dick, hissing as he filled her. Her gorgeous ass pressed snug against his belly, and his cock twitched inside her at the visual. When he turned the vibrator on to a pulsing setting, the rhythmic humming filled the quiet room.

Jess whimpered before he even touched her with it, then nearly shot off him like a rocket when the buzzing connected with her clit. Holding her down with one arm wrapped around her waist, he moved it in steady circles over her as she bucked and rocked her sex on him, squeezing him tight with her inner muscles as she cried out her pleasure in sobbing gasps. Holding back his orgasm through such a tumult of sensation was the most exquisite bliss he'd ever known.

When they were done, after she'd cried out his name and he'd shuddered against her with his face pressed into the back of her neck and his cock buried deep inside her, he held her against him.

They were quiet for a long time while she stroked his arms in lazy motions. Eyes closed, he breathed in the sweet scent of her and tried to regain his emotional footing.

And then she cleared her throat and said in a soft voice, "Nik? What aren't you telling me?"

Chapter Eight

Behind her, Nik stilled. It had taken all of Jess's courage to ask, even though she was sure she knew the answer.

It was her, probably. Maybe he was mad that she wouldn't give him an answer yet, or maybe he was already thinking about leaving on tour. But being this close to him broke her open in a way she'd never experienced, and she couldn't *not* ask.

Because as beautiful, as heart-stoppingly perfect as the sex had been...he was holding back. He'd been too open from the beginning for her not to notice.

He lifted her off his lap and onto the bed beside him. His expression was serious.

"I wasn't sure if I should say anything..." he began, and she held her breath.

"Just tell me." *I can take it. Maybe.*

"Will you come to New York to spend Christmas with me and my family?"

Her stomach lurched. That was *not* what she'd expected him to say. "What?"

He shifted, turning to look her full in the face. The position drew her attention down his magnificent body that seemed to know exactly how to move with hers. "What?" she said again.

His grin lacked some of its usual brightness. "When my mom called earlier, I told her about you. Asked if I could bring you with me."

"Wait, you told your *mom* about me?" Already? Damn, this was going fast. Too fast. But curiosity briefly outweighed terror. "What did she say?"

He gave a light laugh. "She's thrilled, of course. Can't wait to meet you."

Swallowing hard, Jess pushed herself off the mattress and stood. God, her thighs were still wobbly with aftershocks from the very thorough orgasm he'd just given her. "Hang on, I need to clean up."

Even as she ran for the bathroom, she called herself a coward. This was twice now she'd gone to hide after he'd pressed her about the future beyond this third date, and he was too observant not to notice.

But this had gone so far outside the play zone, she had no idea what to do. Feelings were involved, and physical intimacy. Now he wanted to bring family into it? They were only on their third damn date!

And besides, what was the point? This would all be over soon.

In the bathroom mirror, her eyes were wide and scared. She had to calm down, and the only way that would happen would be if she pumped the brakes to stop them from speeding into unknown territory.

Why would he ask her to meet his parents? Family shit was never part of the bargain. She didn't even go see her own family in Chicago for the holidays, so it didn't make any kind of sense for her to fly all the way to New York City to see his. It was ridiculous.

She'd originally agreed to these dates as a temporary thing, never expecting it to go this far. And now that she knew he had a tour coming up, all her fears were confirmed. Three dates, and then, at some point, he would be leaving. *Thanks for the memories, see you never.*

None of it made sense. But she was too heartbroken to sort it out.

After cleaning herself up and wrapping her body in a towel, she took a deep breath, calling on every ounce of sarcasm and confidence she possessed. Then she swung out of the bathroom to break his heart.

"Thanks for the invitation," she said, keeping her tone light and breezy, like he'd asked her to go to the library and not *meet his parents.* "But it would be kind of silly for me to visit your family when I don't even visit my own, you know?"

He sat on the bed in his boxers, his expression utterly blank. The perpetual warmth in his eyes had disappeared.

"Especially since I don't even like Christmas," she added with a forced laugh.

As she said the words, they tasted like a lie in her mouth. After all the work he'd put into showing her a good time this month, she was starting to love all this Christmas stuff. But the memories would always be tied up with him, and what hadn't been.

More painful holiday memories to add to the collection.

Nik stood and nodded once like he agreed, but his eyes had shuttered and all traces of his easy smile had disappeared. "The roads are probably clear by now," he said, his voice flat. "I'm going outside to clean off the car."

He grabbed his clothes and walked past her into the bathroom, shutting the door behind him with a quiet click.

The hollowness spreading inside her said she'd made a very big mistake. She just didn't know which part of it had done the most damage.

———

THE DRIVE back to Los Angeles was made in near silence, aside from Jess's music playlist, a mix of classic jazz and recent hip hop. Nik wanted to ask her about it, but really, what was the point?

Just as he'd feared, she'd rejected his offer. Laughed it off, like she hadn't even taken it seriously. Taken *him* seriously.

From the very beginning, she'd doubted his sincerity, insisting that this was all a game to him. As if he didn't know his own feelings. As if he couldn't tell that he'd never felt this deeply about anyone else.

This was love. Yes, already. The early stages, or so he guessed. He was falling in love with Jess Davenport.

Maybe he should have told her, but again, what was the point? She wouldn't believe him anyway.

Besides, after so much vulnerability and openness, he was exhausted. He just didn't have it in him to bare his soul yet again.

So, they'd packed up, speaking only when necessary, and hit the road.

They were almost back when Dimitri called. Nik answered via the car's Bluetooth.

"Da," he said, then continued in Russian. "You're on speakerphone, and she's in the car with me."

He cut a look at Jess, who kept her eyes down, fiddling with her phone. It was the height of rudeness to talk about someone in another language when they were right there and you knew they couldn't understand, but at the moment, he was too tired to figure out how else to handle what was surely coming.

"Mama said you're bringing your girl home for Christmas."

Yup, there it was. Nik sighed. "Nyet. And she's not my girl."

There was a long pause on Mitya's end. "Oh. Well. Sorry, I guess."

"Me too." He switched lanes as they approached the exit to Jess's neighborhood. "I'll be home soon."

Alone, he wanted to add, but no point heaping his melancholy on Dimitri. Mitya would've done it to him, but he was a drama queen. That just wasn't Nik's style.

He tapped his fingers on the steering wheel as he followed the navigation to Jess's West Hollywood apartment, reconsidering. He'd never been in love before. If there were ever a time to give moping a try, this was it.

He pulled up in front of her apartment complex and swung out of the car, heading for the trunk to get her bags. Just because his feelings were hurt wasn't a reason to drop his manners altogether, and he felt bad about talking about her in Russian with Dimitri while she was still in the car. In hindsight, he could have said he'd call Mitya back. It hadn't occurred to him at the moment. Lack of sleep, the long drive, and heartache were messing with him. He just wanted to get home—well, to his brother's house—and climb into bed.

Yeah, moping sounded pretty damn good.

Jess was waiting behind him when he turned with her suitcase. He set it beside her.

"Have fun with your family," she said, her tone subdued.

"Thanks." What else could he say? *Have fun with your...Netflix?*

"What day do you get back?"

"The twenty-eighth."

She nodded. "Well, text me when you get back to LA. But I don't think we should be in contact while you're gone."

He should've expected something like this. Still, it was like a kick to the gut, leaving him winded and...hurt. But what could he do?

He nodded. "Fine."

————

THERE. She'd said it. The entire ride back, Jess had been trying to think of how to put up some kind of boundary against Nik after he'd so thoroughly demolished her emotional defenses. "No contact" was the best she'd come up with.

"You should focus on your family," she added, as if that would soften the blow. She hated hurting him this way, but she was desperate for some space. The cabin trip had been too much, too fast, too deep. She needed distance to sort out her feelings, and three-thousand miles ought to do the job.

Besides, she could already feel him withdrawing. And that hurt, too.

Nik turned to get back in the car, then stopped. He spoke with his back to her.

"Jess, I need you to understand something. I'm leaving to spend the holidays with my family because that's what I do, and I'm respecting your choice not to do that. You will be alone over Christmas because that was your choice. You've sworn up and down that it's what you want." He turned, and his eyes roiled with emotion. His body fairly vibrated with it. But what was it? Frustration? Anger? Something else?

"So, I'll give that to you," he continued, slashing a hand through the air. "Even though I wish to god you'd come with me, or let me stay with you, I'm going. Alone. Because that's what *you* want."

She swallowed hard. He was right. Nothing he'd just said was a lie. So why did it feel so awful? She tried for bravado. "Don't get it twisted, Nik. You've known this about me from the start."

"You're right." His lips pressed together and his eyes pinched like he was in pain. His voice was tight with emotion, but strong. "But you know what else I know? You mask your feelings with humor. You answer a question with a question. You say you don't want to get into something serious because people play games, but you're the one who's been playing, ever since we started this, because you're too scared to take it seriously. So you tell yourself that I must be playing, too, when the reality is I've never been more serious about anything in my life. So ask yourself, Jess, are you taking life seriously, or are you just playing around?"

She sucked in a breath, stunned silent. *Fuuuuck.* He'd told her.

And she couldn't deny a single word of it. She was still that lonely girl listening to Nina Simone in her tiny bedroom, dreaming of someday making a deeper connection with someone.

Suddenly, only one thing mattered, and she had to get it out before the tears backed up in her throat let loose.

"Will I see you at New Year's?"

Shit, she'd just answered a question with a question. Again. But as much as she needed space from him now, she also needed to see this through to the end, to see him one last time.

Even if their midnight kiss would also be a goodbye.

His shoulders slumped, and he looked absolutely defeated. She'd done this to him. Made this vital, energetic, happy-go-lucky man look so sad and wounded. How had everything gone so wrong?

"Maybe," he finally answered, and it was the confirmation of everything she'd feared from the start.

He wasn't coming back.

He must have accepted the tour. But then, why shouldn't he?

He'd made her believe. Gotten her feelings involved. And now he was leaving for good. Just as she'd known he would. There had never been a real chance for them.

She tried to make her voice light and breezy, to belie how much she was hurting inside. "Well, lemme know if you come back. You know where I'll be. But like I said, I think it's best if we don't contact each other over Christmas. See ya."

The second she turned around, the tears spilled over, and she hurried into her building's lobby, dragging her suitcase. Behind her, the car door opened and slammed.

She took the elevator up to her empty apartment. She'd only been gone one night, but it was like she hadn't been there in months. Everything seemed strange.

And then it hit her. No Christmas decorations.

She took off her shoes and jacket, left the suitcase by the door, and climbed into bed fully dressed.

Already, she missed him. Would it have been so hard to invite him up instead of sending him away?

And then the tears really flowed, because if it had been easy for her, she would have done it. But she hadn't. So, what did that say about her, that she'd run all the way from Chicago to Los Angeles, looking for connection, only to push away the most amazing man she'd ever met?

Chapter Nine

December 24th, Christmas Eve

NIK LOVED CHRISTMAS. And he loved his family. It was wonderful to see his parents, to see Natasha and Dimitri celebrate their first Christmas together, to see Alex and Marina so excited about the upcoming birth of their first child. Christmas in the Kovalenko family meant being surrounded by loving couples, people who had happily settled down because it was worth it when you had the person you loved by your side.

Nik wanted what they had. He'd never noticed the little signs of connection, of love, between the people around him. The way Alex leaped to refill Marina's water glass before she could get up. How Mitya hung on Tash's every word. The way his father came up behind his mother in the kitchen to rest his hands on her shoulders and knead her muscles gently.

Nik wanted all of that and more.

With Jess.

She didn't want any of it, though. Didn't want *him*. She

preferred to stay home, alone, whiling away the holidays watching TV. And when he got back?

Despite her invitation to text her when he returned to LA, he didn't have high hopes. After all, she'd also said they should have no contact while he was gone. She was probably trying to find a way to let him down gently.

His uncle flipped channels, landing for a moment on some version of *A Christmas Carol*.

It reminded Nik of Jess, his adorable Scrooge. He glowered at his uncle and hefted himself up from the sofa, seeking refuge in the kitchen.

"Do you need help with anything, mamochka?" he asked his mother, sticking to English because Natasha stood by her side at the stove. Oksana had been cooking for two days, and tonight they'd have Christmas Eve dinner. Tomorrow, they would drive out to New Jersey to Alex's house for Christmas Day festivities with all the other cousins.

"Start setting the table," his mother told him, pointing at the dishes of food on the counter. "Use the Christmas plates."

He knew the drill. In the dining room, he opened the lower shelves of the china cabinet and carefully unwrapped the good plates they used for Christmas.

When they were kids, this had been Dimitri's job, but early on it became clear that while Nik was a holy terror most of the time, racing up and down the halls in the small apartment they'd shared with his aunt, uncle, and cousins, he took great care with precious items. Slowly and methodically, he set the table the way his mother liked it done, the way she'd taught him so many years before.

His parents had belonged to the Eastern Orthodox Church before coming to America, which celebrated Christmas on January 7th. They'd tried to keep to their traditions, but the public school holiday schedule had made it difficult. When Nik started school, he'd been upset that the other kids celebrated Christmas before he did, and eventually his parents had shifted to celebrating on December 25th. Still, on January 6th and 7th, his family celebrated again with the traditions of their home country. It had meant two Christmases, so Nik had loved it. They also left their tree up until after both celebrations. He'd had a friend in school, Luis, who was Puerto Rican and celebrated Three Kings Day on January 6th. Sometimes they stopped by each other's houses to join in on the additional holiday customs, and it had made Nik feel like it was normal to celebrate on an extra day. Plus, his father's extended family was Jewish, and they had sometimes celebrated Hanukkah with them.

All of these experiences had reinforced the idea that while people might come from different places, by settling in the same place and bringing their traditions with them, they could all come together in the spirit of celebration, family, and love. For him, that was the true meaning of the Christmas season. It wasn't about religion, or spending money, or even about the particular holiday of Christmas itself. It was about connection. The days were getting longer again, bit by bit, and Christmas was about opening yourself up to that light and letting people in.

Through all three dates with Jess, that's what he'd tried to show her. It was okay to let people in.

His phone felt heavy in his back pocket, and his fingers itched to text her. But what would he say?

Let me in. Please.

He couldn't. And anyway, he knew what her answer would be.

When he returned to the kitchen for the food, his mother stopped him and pressed her hands to his cheeks. "Moy mal'chik," she crooned, then spoke in English. "You are so sad, Kolya. It breaks my heart that you won't tell me what happened."

No one laid on a guilt trip like his mother. She'd even busted out his childhood nickname. He met Natasha's eyes over Oksana's head for a brief second. Tash gave a little headshake, which he took to mean his mother had drilled her for info and she hadn't told.

He just shrugged and said, "It didn't work out."

It was what he'd said the other twenty times his mother had

questioned him since he'd walked in the front door the previous day. If he could go back, he wouldn't have mentioned Jess at all.

"I have to put out the food," he mumbled, slipping away from his mother's intense gaze. Hefting a large tray of pierogis, he ducked out of the kitchen.

What was he supposed to say? He'd tried. He'd gone big with Jess, as big as he could go, and then...he'd gone home.

Not enough.

The thought made him pause. He set the platter down in the center of the dining room table, then snagged a pierogi off it and nibbled.

The comforting taste of peppery potato and dough always brought him back to childhood, and the feeling of being home. Yet it did nothing to dispel the sick feeling that everything he'd done, everything he was, wasn't enough for Jess. He'd laid it all on the line, given her his heart, and it wasn't enough.

He gulped down the rest of the pierogi so his mom didn't catch him snacking before dinner. Another option floated through his mind. Maybe it wasn't too late to take the *Raise Your Voice* role, or find another tour contract.

What would be worse—staying in Los Angeles and feeling like a third wheel in his brother's house, or returning to work feeling like an absolute failure?

Neither option appealed. He'd feel like a failure either way.

He shook it off, tried to paste a smile he didn't feel to his face, and returned to his mother's kitchen.

Chapter Ten

December 25th, Christmas Day

I nstead of feeling excited to spend some quality "me time" with herself, Jess woke on Christmas Day with a stomachache that had nothing to do with the cookies she'd eaten the night before— leftover from the decorating party at Dimitri's house—and everything to do with the fact that Nik had been right. She was alone on Christmas because she had chosen to be. She was alone *period* because she'd chosen to be. And for the first time, she was questioning why that was.

For that, she needed caffeine.

She rolled out of bed, made herself a cup of coffee in the kitchen, and sat down in the front of the TV to drink.

This had been her plan, after all. Spend the holidays relaxing and catching up on the shows she'd missed while filming *The Dance Off*. Her poor, neglected DVR was calling her name.

But something stopped her from turning on the TV. Christmas, something she'd told herself multiple times was just another day in the year, seemed to have some sway over her. And she couldn't just sit here watching a historical time travel drama like it was any old day. Even if it didn't mean much to her, personally, Christmas meant something to other people.

She finished her coffee, took a shower, then looked for something comfortable to wear. She still didn't own anything Christmas themed, but—no wait, she did! She still had Lorena's poinsettia earrings and Naomi's "Lit As a Christmas Tree" t-shirt, which she'd washed but hadn't yet returned. She paired the borrowed items with dark wash jeans and ankle boots. The weather had finally gotten the memo that it was winter, and the high was only fifty-three degrees. In Southern California, that was wool coat and Uggs weather. She spritzed her hair with water, then sealed it with a coconut hair oil. And since she was adhering to a theme, she applied Holly Jolly Berry to her lips. It had become her new favorite lipstick.

As she drove, she wondered what Nik was doing with his family. Eating? Opening presents? Singing carols or watching classic Christmas movies? Her own family Christmas traditions involved opening presents during breakfast before a trip to church. Did his family go to church? She hadn't even asked. It had been years since she'd stepped foot inside one.

Since it was on her mind, she had the car call her parents' house phone.

Her mother's sweet, resonant voice rang out from the speakers, bright with surprise. "Well, hi, baby!"

"Hi, Mommy. Merry Christmas."

"Thanks, baby. I'm so glad you called." Then, in a muffled tone, she called out, "Roy, Jess is on the phone. Pick up in the other room."

She'd shown them how to use the speakerphone, but it hadn't stuck. It hit her then that her parents, for the most part, always called her first. Always said "happy birthday" or "merry Christmas" first. Her childhood hadn't been easy, certainly, but it hadn't been all bad, and she knew they loved her.

New Year's Resolution #1: Call her parents more often.

Her dad's voice jumped in. "Are you doing anything fun today, Jessie?"

"Hey, Daddy. I'm going to Starlight House to help out."

"Oh, that's a lovely thing to do," her mom said. "And what about that boy from the dancing video?"

Jess tried to keep her tone light. "Um, I don't know what he's up to. We're just friends."

Were they even that now? And it was a lie—she did know what he was up to. She might not know what he was doing that very moment, but she knew he was celebrating Christmas, surrounded by his family.

As her mom detailed what she was making for dinner and her dad shared all his thoughts on the latest blockbuster action movie, Jess wondered if maybe she'd been holding onto old anger for a bit too long.

Her parents were people. People had flaws. They had their own bullshit that got in the way sometimes. But they weren't evil. Had their flaws affected her childhood? Yes. But how long was she going to make them guilty for that? She was an adult now. It was time she stopped blaming her parents for her own unhappiness.

And her own poor relationship choices.

It was too late now, but maybe next year she'd visit them for the holidays.

For now, she was going to do the next best thing.

She said goodbye to her parents and parked in the small lot outside Starlight House. From here, she could appreciate the effort they'd made to decorate. Pine boughs and holly outlined the front doors, woven with twinkling white lights. The sky above was overcast, but was due to clear up as the day went on. She swung out of the car and headed for the front doors.

Inside, the lobby contained an explosion of decorations. A tree stood in front of each window, trimmed with a combo of handmade and store-bought ornaments. Icicle lights hung from the ceiling, and the desk was draped with tinsel. They'd been busy since her last visit.

Nik would have liked it.

The thought gave her a pang. She brushed it aside and went up to the older woman sitting behind the front desk. "Hey, Mrs. Fernandez," she said with a wave.

Mrs. Fernandez looked up from the novel she was reading, blinking at Jess over the tops of her glasses. "Oh, good morning, Jess! Merry Christmas."

"Merry Christmas," Jess replied. "I heard you all were on a skeleton staff this week, so I thought I'd come by to help."

Mrs. Fernandez's expression softened. "That's very kind of you. I'm sure the girls will be happy to see you. They're in the dining hall having breakfast. Naomi's in there, too."

"Really?" She hadn't thought Naomi would be in today, since her family lived just a few hours' drive south in San Diego. "Thanks, Mrs. F."

She heard the sounds of celebration from the hallway. Laughing, talking, footsteps squeaking on linoleum, and, of course, Christmas carols.

Jess entered the room as the speakers sang out, "In the meadow we can build a snowman," and her thoughts turned to Nik once again.

Was it snowing in New York? Had their own snowchild melted up on Big Bear?

"Well, well, well, fancy seeing you here." Naomi appeared at her side and gave Jess a hip bump. "Got bored with all that relaxing?"

Jess shot her a look, but it must have been more mopey than menacing, because Naomi's face converted into a mask of concern.

"Oh, babe." She put an arm around Jess's shoulders and didn't even comment on the t-shirt. "What's going on? Is it Nik?"

Jess nodded, then shook her head. "Yeah. I'm all mixed up. I don't think I can talk about it right now." *Or think about it.*

Naomi gave her a squeeze. "You know I'm here for you, whenever you're ready."

As a counselor, Naomi was probably the best person to talk

with, but Jess was always careful not to overstep the bonds of friendship in that way. She never wanted Naomi to feel like she was using her.

But she was so confused, maybe it would be good to talk it out. Friend to friend.

Later, though. Today, it was Christmas. And here, unlike in her apartment, that meant something.

For the rest of the day, Jess buried herself in work in an effort not to think about Nik. But it didn't help. For one thing, being with the girls at Starlight House didn't feel like work. She genuinely enjoyed spending time with them, teaching them dance moves, organizing arts and crafts activities, and managing cleanup. An anonymous benefactor had made a massive last-minute donation of beautifully wrapped gifts, and she derived great joy from passing them out and watching the girls marvel over their presents. Most of these kids were victims of trauma, and it warmed Jess's heart to see them happy.

Still, in the back of her mind, a little voice pointed out that it would've been even better if Nik were there. He'd be kind to these girls, showing them the model of a man who was good and upstanding. And any man willing to eat a phallus-shaped cookie just to make her laugh would go all out bringing holiday cheer to Starlight.

And, if she were being one hundred percent honest with herself, she just plain missed him. She missed his voice. His touch. The way he asked her questions like he genuinely wondered about what made her tick, then listened carefully to the answers, filing them away and surprising her when he referenced them later. He was a man who cared, and who took care with everyone and everything he encountered.

Despite her worries that he was just messing around with her, he'd been nothing but reliable and respectful.

Even now, he was respecting her wishes not to be contacted.

She sighed, and wished that in this one instance, he'd go against her decree and reach out.

More than that, she wished he were here. But he wasn't. And that was her own doing.

———

AT ALEX'S HOUSE, Nik did his best to be his usual, upbeat self, but it wasn't working. His mother had stopped asking about Jess, Natasha and Marina eyed him with open concern, and Alex and Dimitri hadn't teased him once. His dad had even patted his back and given him the Russian equivalent of, "Good job, son."

When he'd asked, "What was that for?" his dad just nodded and left the room.

Even his other cousins tiptoed around him with none of their usual good-natured teasing. Mitya had probably texted them all something like, *Nik's going through his first heartbreak, so don't be assholes to him, okay?*

After breakfast, Nik sat in the family room, watching his cousin Fedya's children tear into their new toys. They were sweet kids, and they reminded him of the way he'd played with his brother and cousins when they were that age.

Little Inessa struggled to open a Barbie box while her brothers ignored her, so Nik waved her over. "Idi syuda, Nessa. I'll help you."

Lower lip quivering, the little girl tottered over and climbed into his lap before handing him the box. In a soothing voice, he described each step as he opened it and detached the Barbie from her cardboard backing.

"See?" he said in English. "And then we just untwist this last tie here, and…ta-da!"

"Barbie!" Inessa trilled. She took the doll, leaving him covered in more packaging than could possibly be necessary for an eleven-inch computer programmer doll, and went back to sit on the floor by the tree.

"Well done." Dimitri clapped from the doorway, then plopped onto the sofa next to Nik. "So, how's Jess?"

"I don't know." Nik tried to shift away, but his brother didn't let up.

"You ready to talk about it?"

Letting out an exasperated breath, Nik crossed his arms over his chest. "She wanted to spend Christmas alone." Even to his own ears, he sounded petulant. "She told me from the beginning she likes to be alone. I should've listened."

Mitya waved that away. "People always say stuff they don't really mean when it comes to love."

"I don't think she's lying about it."

"She might not be. Maybe she does like being alone. The real question is *why* she likes to be alone. And if you can figure out the why, and solve the *real* problem, maybe she'll be okay with letting you in. Besides, it's only been a few weeks. People need time to discover what's in their hearts. Look how long it took me and Tasha."

Nik considered Mitya's words. It was true that Mitya and Tash had danced around each other—literally and figuratively—for a few years before finally becoming an item, and now it was like Natasha had always been part of the family. For Nik, he'd been thinking about Jess all year, and had known since this summer that he'd wanted to give a relationship with her a shot once his tour ended. But for Jess, it had only been a couple weeks, and he'd been rushing her along since day one. Of course she'd balked at flying across the country to visit his parents.

Jess wasn't forthcoming with information about her past, but she'd dropped enough hints that if he fit all the puzzle pieces together, they created a full picture. She liked to be alone because she was afraid of getting hurt. Why? Because she'd been hurt before. How many times had she said it, plain as day? "People are always playing games." She thought he was going to toy with her heart then drop her, like the other guys she'd dated had. Or worse, that he'd up and leave, like her dad.

He had to let her know, in no uncertain terms, that she meant something to him. That he cared about her. Loved her. And he was willing to give it a shot for the long haul, however far she wanted it to go.

But how? He'd agreed to no contact, and he didn't want to step on her boundaries.

The need to reach out to her, just to let her know he was thinking about her, that she wasn't truly alone on this day, or at least, she was only as alone as she wanted to be, drove him off the sofa and into the hallway.

"Hey, where're you going?" Mitya called, but Nik ignored him. His mind raced through all the possible things he could text her, from cute to heartfelt to funny. In the end, he settled on the one obvious choice.

Leaning against the wall in the darkened hallway, he typed out, "Merry Christmas, milochka."

For him, it was the equivalent of "I love you." She'd either get that or she wouldn't. But soon enough, he'd be back in LA.

They still had a plan for New Year's Eve. He had to make it count.

———

AFTER LUNCH, Jess helped set out trays of cookies in the rec room for the girls to munch on while they played with their new gifts or watched the Christmas movie playing on the big TV. She'd helped raise the money to renovate this room the previous year, and every time she was there, she admired the changes. Before, it had looked like the common room at a college dorm—thin carpeting, ugly furniture that was sturdy but uncomfortable, an old TV that wasn't even a flatscreen, and a DVD player that was always on the fritz. Now, it looked inviting and homey, with new electronics, comfy furniture, and a magenta and teal color scheme with ornate faux-gold accents. The girls loved it.

Since there was nothing else to be done at the moment, Jess selected a chocolate chip cookie and took a bite. In her pocket, her phone buzzed. Probably another "Merry Christmas" text from someone she hadn't heard from since last Christmas.

She pulled out the phone and checked the text message on the screen. Yes, it was a holiday greeting, but this one made her breath catch.

Merry Christmas, milochka.

Heart pounding, she set the cookie on a napkin and opened the search app on her phone. She'd heard Nik call her this before, but she hadn't known how to spell it.

She typed in "milochka means" and hit Go.

When the answer appeared, she got a warm feeling all over.

Dearie.

It was sweet, and kind of old fashioned, which fit the two of them so perfectly. Nik with his gallant manners, and her with her love of classic jazz and old movies.

Maybe it wasn't over yet. If he was still thinking about her, that meant she still had a chance to fix things. After all, it wasn't over until the final curtain call—in this case, Dimitri's New Year's Eve party.

"Miss Jessica?"

Jess shut off her phone and looked up. It was Tamara, one of the younger girls in the house.

"What's up, Tam-Tam?" she asked, using the girl's nickname.

Tamara gestured at a group of three girls fiddling with the sound system. "Can you help us choreograph a dance?"

"Of course I can!"

As Jess helped them put together a sequence of dance moves to a Christmas pop song, a few more girls joined them. And sometime between choreographing the steps and running through the routine all together, Jess was hit with an epiphany.

While the girls took a cookie break, Jess pulled out her phone and shot back a text to Nik.

It was time to take a chance.

Chapter Eleven

December 28th

hree days later, Jess stood outside Starlight House again, battling a rollicking case of anxiety. Nik's SUV pulled into the lot, and she bit her lip while she waited for him to join her.

God, she'd missed him. That smooth swagger, those warm brown eyes, his hair just a little wild and ten kinds of sexy.

Inside, all she could think was, *You came back*. And it filled her with warm, gooey feelings she couldn't yet name.

When he approached, she launched into business mode to keep from throwing herself at him.

"This is Starlight House," she said by way of greeting, holding open the front door so he could enter. "It has been serving adolescent girls who are labeled as at-risk or victims of trauma since its founding in 1985. In 2016, it was updated to meet California's new model for group homes, the Short Term Residential Therapeutic Programs model."

He looked around, taking in the decorations that were still up. When he met her eyes again, Jess pressed a hand to her chest. "I asked you to meet me here because this is the most special place on earth to me. When I talk about settling down, it's not just out of complacency or comfort. It's about growing roots. This place is part of that."

His eyes softened as he listened, his focus intent on her. It was how he always looked at her when she talked. He listened, deeply. So, even though it was hard to reveal so much of herself like this, she kept going.

"Growing up in Chicago, I relied on community centers and free programs to further my interest and education in dance. When I heard about this place, I knew it was my chance to give back. Because for me, settling down is also about getting involved in the community."

His silence was starting to unnerve her. Hell, she hadn't even given him the chance to say hello. But her mouth kept going as her nerves hit the "ramble" button. "I wanted you to see this place, because it's as much a part of me as *The Dance Off*, and you only know that side of me. And, well, because…I guess I want you to know all sides of me."

Ugh, what a dumb ending. Why hadn't she rehearsed what she wanted to say?

Just then, Mrs. Fernandez entered the lobby. When she saw them, her face lit up. "Oh, Mr. Kovalenko. Thank you so much for the gifts you sent. They really made the girls' Christmas that much more special."

Jess froze. The gifts? Nik had sent them?

Nik inclined his head, full of gallantry. "It was my pleasure."

"Is Jess giving you the tour?" Mrs. F asked.

Smiling at Jess, Nik nodded. "She is."

It was all Jess could do to keep a straight face. Her mind reeled at the revelation.

"Great." Mrs. F took her seat behind the desk. "She's been volunteering here for a few years, and she's initiated some excellent fundraising efforts, as well as therapeutic dance classes for the girls."

"She's a gem," he murmured.

Clutching his elbow, Jess beamed a smile at the older woman, then propelled Nik into the hallway so they could have some privacy.

Once they were alone, she released his arm and stared up at him. "You knew?"

"Of course. You post about this place on Instagram all the time. Since I didn't think you'd want me buying you a Christmas present, I sent gifts here instead. It seemed like that would mean more to you anyway, and besides, Christmas is about community and giving back."

Inside, her heart shattered, then reformed. When she spoke, her voice was tight with emotion. "I don't know how to thank you. I was here when they opened the presents. I wish you could have seen the joy on their faces, the fun they were having."

His lips twisted, and there was something wistful in his eyes. "There's always next year," he said softly.

All traces of doubt she'd ever held about him vanished. This man was kind, conscientious, and most of all, understood her need to stick around and give back. He *was* serious, and he wasn't playing games with her.

She could trust him.

He took her hand, holding it gently. "Jeshka, I...I'm sorry I rushed you."

She opened her mouth to contradict, to thank him for rushing because moving fast was the only way to bypass her defenses before she could create new ones, and really, yes, she *did* want this, when someone else spoke.

"There you are."

Their heads snapped up to where Naomi strode down the hall toward them with a big smile on her face.

Jess handled the introduction. "Nik, this is Naomi. She's one of the counselors here."

Nik shook her hand. "I remember seeing you at Rhianne's party. I'm sorry I didn't introduce myself properly then."

Naomi chuckled. "No worries. Your mind was busy. Thanks again for the gifts you sent."

"It was my pleasure."

Then she turned to Jess. "Before you get started, I have some news."

Jess frowned, hoping nothing had gone wrong with the day's plans. "What kind of news?"

"Don't worry, it's good news. We want you to join the Starlight House board."

Jess's pulse thumped, sure she'd misheard. "The what?"

"The board!" Naomi pulled Jess into a hug. "You've done so much over the last year, between fundraising efforts and donating your time to teach and hang out with the girls. So, you're officially being invited to join the board of directors to help ensure Starlight keeps moving in a good direction."

Wow. Board of directors. Part of her felt like she was too young for such a responsibility, but Starlight House and the girls it served meant the world to her, and the thought of stepping into a more official role and being able to help even more gave her a feeling of…rightness. Yes, this was the kind of thing she'd been looking to do more of.

"I'm…I'm speechless." Jess hugged Naomi back. "And honored. Thank you."

"That's wonderful news, Jeshka," Nik said quietly at her side, and Jess turned to see him beaming a proud smile at her. She was so happy, both from Naomi's news and just from having Nik here with her, she wanted to throw herself into his arms and squeeze him tight. But if she did, Naomi would tease her mercilessly.

Oh, what the hell.

Jess wrapped her arms around Nik's midsection and hugged him hard. When he enveloped her in his warm, solid embrace and his spicy-sweet scent, she was sure she'd never felt anything so perfect.

When she released him, Naomi didn't laugh, but she did gesture down the hallway.

"By the way, everything is set up. We're ready when you are."

When Nik shot Jess a curious look, she slapped a hand to her forehead. "Shit. I forgot to mention one other thing."

"What's that?"

"I told everyone you were stopping by to teach a dance class. The girls are very excited, so you can't say no."

"Teaching with you?"

Of course he'd focus on that part. "Yeah."

His face lit up, and he didn't ask any more questions. Slinging an arm around her shoulders to tuck her in against his side, he smiled down at her. "I'd love to."

Chapter Twelve

December 31st, New Year's Eve

Nik had a lot to do before the end of the year, and as Dimitri's New Year's Eve party approached, anxiety kicked in.

Even after everything Jess had said at Starlight House, and how much fun they'd had teaching the dance class together, he wouldn't feel fully settled until she kissed him at midnight. That was the symbol they'd agreed upon, signifying continued commitment.

Guests started arriving at nine. Nik hung around by the front door, greeting everyone, but he was really waiting for Jess. The longer the night went on, the more his nerves frayed. What if she wasn't coming? He nursed a single beer, mostly to have something in his hands, and checked his phone compulsively for texts. His mind replayed every moment they'd spent together, looking for clues as to what had gone wrong, but when they'd parted ways at Starlight House, everything had seemed settled.

There was that word again. *Settled.*

He didn't feel settled now. Had he missed her entrance? He

roamed the party, searching for her, before resuming his spot by the front door again.

It was almost midnight and he was going out of his mind with worry when Natasha rushed up to him, looking frazzled. "Nik, I need you to go in the kitchen and check on catering. They're having a champagne fiasco."

"What do you mean?" he asked, frowning. The catering team was from the restaurant Dimitri owned, and he couldn't imagine they'd dare to have any kind of fiasco in their boss's house.

She threw up her hands. "I don't know. Go check!"

"I got it, sestra. Don't worry." This was Natasha's first time acting as hostess in Dimitri's home, and she'd been more than a little stressed leading up to the party. Nik patted her shoulder and made a beeline for the kitchen.

In the kitchen doorway, Nik froze, and belatedly remembered that the catering team was set up in the garage.

Jess sat on the counter, legs swinging gently. She hunched her shoulders and gave him a little wave. "Hi."

"Hi yourself," he said, turning her own words back on her from just a couple weeks ago. How could it have been such a short amount of time? His whole world had changed.

He glanced at the microwave clock. 11:57. "Cutting it a little close, aren't you?"

She sent him a cheeky grin, her dimple flashing. "Would it be mean of me to say I wanted you to sweat a little?"

"Yes. Very."

"Does that mean you were sweating?"

"Absolutely. I've been hanging out by the door all night." He held up the beer bottle. "This has been warm for two hours."

"Gross." Her eyes twinkled at him with good humor. Then she pulled a chilled bottle of champagne from an ice bucket behind her and held it up. "Maybe you should have some of this instead."

So, this had been the champagne fiasco Natasha had referred to. "Did Tash let you in through the garage?"

"Yeah, I texted her. Rhianne drove me and Natasha helped me sneak in."

He walked over, took the bottle, and drank deep.

She laughed. "Dude, you're not supposed to chug the good shit."

He swallowed and caught his breath. "I've been stressed."

"Oh yeah? Why's that?" Her smile turned smug.

"I think you know why."

Her tone softened. "Because you've been trying to woo a Scrooge who didn't believe in love or Christmas?"

"Something like that." He moved into the space between her knees and gave her the champagne. "I've also been running all over Los Angeles for three days looking at real estate. We made an offer yesterday morning and it was accepted today. Lucky for me, my big brother is a movie star and incredibly pushy."

She paused with the bottle halfway to her lips. "You did what?"

"Bought a house." He gestured around them. "Can't live with Mitya forever."

From outside, the countdown chant began. *Thirty, twenty-nine…*

"Why don't they just start at ten?" she asked, but her voice was dreamy and her eyes were transfixed on his.

"Dimitri likes the anticipation. Besides, it gives people time to find someone to kiss."

"Sounds like a good plan." She took a swig of champagne, then passed the bottle back to him.

Fifteen, fourteen…

Nik set the champagne aside and cupped her cheek.

"Jess?"

"Mmm?"

"Why did you kiss me back? A year ago."

"Oh." Her lashes fluttered closed. "Because you asked. You didn't just take."

Nine, eight…

"Nik?"

"Yeah?"

She let out a trembling breath. "I want you to stay."

Those five words were the best thing he'd ever heard. Inside him, the final missing piece clicked into place.

Three, two…

"Begin as you mean to go on," he whispered against her lips.

One! Happy new year!

Amid the sound of cheers and noisemakers from the backyard, Nik kissed her long and deep, with all the love in his heart. Jess clung to him tightly, her mouth soft and lush under his, pulling him closer until their hearts beat against each other.

"Does this mean you'll stay?" she asked when their lips broke apart, hope and her heart shining in her eyes.

"Jeshka, I *bought* a *house*."

"But what about your tour?"

"I already turned it down."

She gasped, eyes widening. "What? When?"

"While we were at the cabin."

"Nik." She shook her head at him, but couldn't hide her smile. "You could've told me that and saved us both a lot of heartache."

"And you could have just told me you wanted me to stay." He framed her face with his hands, stroking her soft skin with gentle movements. "Besides, I needed you to trust that I meant it, otherwise you'd keep worrying I was going to leave."

"Okay, true. But you were going to stay anyway!"

"Yeah, just in case you needed more than three dates."

She snuggled in against his chest. "Well, it turns out I do."

"How many more?" He wrapped her in his arms.

"Infinity dates."

"You got it, milochka."

She gave him another kiss, then tugged on his hand. "Now come on. I've been waiting to dance with you all night."

Epilogue

January 6th

The "fasten seatbelt" icon lit up with a *ding*, and Jess buckled in as the plane prepared for takeoff. "I'm nervous."

Nik patted her hand. "She'll love you."

"How do you know that?"

"Because I do."

Her cheeks warmed and she smiled down into her lap. Over the last week, Nik had become very free with the L word, and... hell, who was she kidding? She fucking loved it.

Being suddenly part of a couple was weird, but nice. More than nice. They spent time together at her apartment, watching old movies; at Dimitri's house, lounging in the hot tub or practicing in Dimitri's private dance studio; and at Starlight House, teaching classes or just helping out. They made decisions together, exploring furniture stores and building Pinterest boards for Nik's new house. Jess wasn't moving in with him—despite his invitation that she do so whenever she felt ready—but she thought she might when her lease was up in a few months. Nik would even be joining her in Vancouver to film the Heartflix movie. The production team had reached out to offer him a guest spot as her dance partner in the scene, although Jess wondered if Lorena had something to do with that.

And now, they were visiting his family together.

"Tell me more about Ukrainian Christmas," she said. "And about your mom. And your dad. And your cousin."

"Cousins," he corrected. "But there are a lot of them, and I don't expect you to remember all their names."

"Fine. Your parents, then. Natasha says they're really nice."

"They are. They'll be nice to you, in any case. Sometimes they still try to baby me."

"You're the youngest. It goes with the territory."

"We'll do a full Ukrainian Christmas Eve dinner tonight," he told her. "Just us and my parents. Tomorrow Alex and Marina— she's the pregnant one—will come by, along with my cousin Fedya and his family."

"Fedya?"

"Short for Fyodor. Everyone has a nickname."

"Like how you call me Jeshka." She loved that he'd made her name sound special. She'd gone to school with so many other Jessicas, Jessies, and Jesses, by sixth grade the other kids just called her Davenport. "Or milochka."

He nodded. "Although maybe it's time I gave you a new nickname."

"Like what?" She leaned in, eager to hear what he came up with.

Pink bloomed on his cheeks, and her heart flip-flopped. His blushes were so damn cute!

"Lyubimaya," he muttered, the word musical and enchanting to her ears.

"What does it mean?" she asked in a hushed voice as the flight attendant swept by, closing the overhead compartments.

His gaze met hers. "Beloved."

"Oh." Now her cheeks got warm. "I like it."

"Me too."

She took a deep breath, let it out slow. "Actually…I love it."

Maybe he got what she was really trying to say, because he caught her chin and kissed her, slow and sensual. When he raised his head, he whispered, "I love it, too."

Author's Note

Dear Reader,

I swear, I meant to write Kevin's book next. But time and deadlines wait for no writer, and I somehow found myself slipping a Dance Off holiday story into my writing schedule instead.

When I sat down to develop the idea, Nik and Jess's story was just there, as if it had been waiting for me to find it. Their characters took shape quickly, even though they'd only had small mentions in the previous books, and the writing flowed. Watching their love story unfold on the page before me was a delight, and I hope you felt the same while reading it.

Dance All Night also marks me dipping my toe into the waters of indie publishing, so thank you for picking up this title! If you feel so inclined, I'd love it if you dropped me a review.

The best way to stay up to date with future Dance Off news is to subscribe to my newsletter. The Extras tab on my website has the Dance Off cast page and additional scenes, if you're looking for more to read. You can also check out the *Dance All Night* playlist on Spotify.

Again, thank you so much for picking up this story.

All the best,
Alexis

Series Info

If you're new to the Dance Off series, start at the beginning with *Take the Lead: A Dance Off Novel* (#1):

Gina refuses to compromise her reputation for ratings.
Stone will do anything to hide his family's secrets.
Is passion enough to keep the city girl and the survivalist together?

Also check out *Dance with Me: A Dance Off Novel* (#2):

All Natasha ever wanted is to make it as a dancer.
Dimitri just wants to win her heart.
Is their off-the-charts chemistry enough to risk career-ruining rumors?

Coming Soon

Feel the Rhythm: A Dance Off Novel (#3) coming in 2019!

Acknowledgments

This book was conceived and written in a whirlwind. First and foremost, thanks goes to my amazing agent, Sarah E. Younger. I couldn't have done this without her, and I send my immense thanks to Sarah and the team at NYLA for bringing this story to the world.

I also wouldn't have gotten this done without the help of my wonderful editor, Holly Ingraham, and my fabulous copyeditor, Lindsey Faber. They've been with me on this series since the beginning, and knowing I had their support while publishing this novella made the whole process go more smoothly.

To my early readers who also happen to be super talented writers: C.L. Polk, Christina Hovland, Sarah Morgenthaler, LaQuette, Scarlett Peckham, and Robin Lovett—thank you all for the feedback. Special thanks to Susannah Erwin for the Christmas in Los Angeles details, Katrina L. and Sarah M. for their help with the Russian words used in this book, and Elizabeth Mahon for sharing her wealth of ballroom dance knowledge.

To my Golden Heart Rebelles, thank you for sparking the idea of a holiday novella in the first place! And to my RWA-NYC, 4 Chicas Chat, and Team RWchat groups, thank you all for supporting me as I threw myself headfirst into this endeavor. (And thanks to everyone for looking at multiple cover designs without complaining.)

To my readers—and I feel so grateful that I can even say that—thank you for taking a chance on me and this series, and huge thanks to everyone who has reached out to let me know they read and enjoyed the previous books. It means more than I can ever say.

Thanks to my family and friends for understanding when I once again disappeared to work on a book. And thanks to my boyfriend for always being there for me, and for literally building a new computer so I could finish designing the cover.

Also by Alexis Daria

Dance Off Series

Take the Lead

Dance with Me

Dance All Night: A Dance Off Holiday Novella

Feel the Rhythm

Solstice Miracle (free holiday short story!)

About the Author

Alexis Daria is an award-winning contemporary romance author, artist, and native New Yorker. Her debut, TAKE THE LEAD, was a 2018 RITA® Award winner for "Best First Book" and was named one of the Best Romance Novels of 2017 by *The Washington Post* and *Entertainment Weekly*. Alexis has a BFA in Computer Arts, but her most fulfilling job was as a group facilitator for a women's empowerment community, where she coached other women in following their creative dreams. She loves social media, and you can find her live-tweeting her favorite TV shows at @alexisdaria, or talking about writing and books on her blog at alexisdaria.com. Sign up for her newsletter for access to exclusive bonus content: http://bit.ly/2wquDD1.

Twitter: @alexisdaria
Facebook: /alexisdaria1
Facebook group: 4 Chicas Chat
Instagram: @alexisdaria
Pinterest: @alexisdaria

CPSIA information can be obtained
at www.ICGtesting.com
Printed in the USA
FSHW012157151218
54485FS